The Sunset Honeymoon

By

Elisha Otieno

Folks! Prepare your souls for departure; we're in trouble!

The village healer shivers! From the haze of a deadly wind blowing across the globe! Plucking the unripe fruits of plants! Breaking the shields of our soldiers! Breaking the walls of our boundaries! Destroying the seeds of our offspring! But the God of our ancestors, at the helm on His throne, casts a shadow on His creation!

Ariba Book Publishers

P.O Box 503-40600

Siaya –Kenya

Website: www.aribabp.com

Email: admin@aribabp.com

ISBN: 978-9966-1856-1-7

Edited by: Collins Odhiambo

Alyp Writers Organisation

First published 2015

CHAPTER ONE

"WHOSE STONE IS THAT?" Adoyo asked, her hoarse, troubled voice conveying the frustration she was suffering in trying to cope with frenzied roommates. She wriggled in bitterness, complaining about perpetual damages caused to the roof of her late mother's grass thatched kitchen, used by maidens from the entire Nyakonja village as their sleeping place, a safe haven for illicit deals with lovers.

Interfering with her peers' private lives was none of Adoyo's business, but their wishy-washy relationships were violating her right to peaceful sleep. She especially could not stomach the thought of modern boys, living in a civilised world, opting for the retrogressive habit of throwing stones at the roof as a way of communicating to their girlfriends. She spoke her mind out aloud.

"Look for yours!" Akelo, rising from the mattress to respond to the call said in reaction to Adoyo's complaints. She got out of the kitchen, leaving the door ajar.

Apisy, the youngest of the bevy of beauties lying on the mattress, sprang up. She jumped over the others, almost stepping on Adoyo's head, slammed the door shut and went to the window, craned her neck and peeped through a slit to take a glimpse of Akelo and her man who were now swapping courtesies and words of love in the banana grove behind the kitchen.

"*Choke!*" Apisy exclaimed. "It's her luminous boyfriend from Alara!"

"Your agemates are asleep!" admonished Amami, Adoyo's cousin, a great player in the love deals.

Apisy stopped it but remained there. Banana leaves rippled in the soft wind as the couple vanished in the inky darkness of the night, leaving an atmosphere of calm in the surrounding.

The village girls hustled around every time the sun sank, courtesy of irresponsible male partners offering short lived, withered romantic relationships. The young men, who were free of parental responsibilities and long-term engagements, hooked up with them, giving big empty promises and whispering sweet nothing to their ears. And the village bimbo is bound to succumb, to every such rabbit endowed with the ego of an elephant.

The high sound of baying dogs across the village was like a farewell message to Akelo and her hunter, wishing the rest a peaceful night.

Adoyo had become the village punching bag. She was on the receiving end of all critics. Hate speeches and threats were directed towards her. However, she stuck to her guns.

She maintained a high level of moral demeanour that placed her at the helm of regulating peoples' behaviour. Her dad, Akondo, the right man to approach on issues pertaining to maintenance of family's social fabric and property, was too engrossed in another new relationship to concentrate on family matters. After all, his children were grown-ups and didn't need his support.

The sons had gone to the urban centers to work for a living, while his daughters were well settled with their hubbies in their respective matrimonial homes. Sadly though, Akondo had lost four of his children. Adoyo, his last-born daughter, now in her early twenties, remained the only biological child around him.

Akondo argued that when the suckers of a banana plant sprout and bear fruits, there is no problem if the main plant itself is cut away. These then provide enough resources to feed the community. He preached such arguments to defend his life choices. He highly cherished life with Akuom, a widow to his cousin. Adoyo abhorred her father's way of reasoning. She regretted her mother's death.

Apart from the frail couple, Akondo and Akuom that developed a romantic relationship in their sunset years, other couples although younger, shrank their life expectancy by engaging in irresponsible sexual behaviour backed by the culture of widow inheritance at a time when the deadly HIV infections intensified, converting the young blood into overnight octogenarians. Couples that defied the use of HIV drugs and other approved precautions, both old and young were equally involved in the sunset honeymoon, a romantic relationship enjoyed by the graveside, expecting the axe of death to cut them down any time sooner as a result of HIV related infections or age for grannies who re-married in their sunset years, relationships celebrated with burial gowns in the name of wedding gowns.

CHAPTER TWO

The scorching heat of the sun roasted Akondo's glittering bald, almost ripping off his scalp. He bit his tongue with rage, a stockpile of fire in his stomach burning his body allover over remarks made to a community elder by his daughter, Adoyo.

"What did she say?" Akuom raised her concern, turning her face to his side in bewilderment.

"Who does she think she is?" he ignored the question and fumed. "Her agemates are long married, but she sticks to her parental home like a tethered cow."

"Kindly tell me what Adoyo said about us," Akuom insisted.

"What should we do to a child who pries into her dad's private life?" Akondo asked.

He choked on his saliva and coughed severely as if his daughter's remarks had some acidic gases in them. He stooped to his walking stick and supported his chin with a gesture that made him look like the famous Nyamgondho statue.

"Come over please. I want to discuss something with you," he whispered with a beckon, leading his lover to a shade by the roadside, out of the vicinity of passersby.

"If it was not you…! I tell you, my dear, if it was not you…!" Akondo spoke with determination, biting his lips and pointing at his lover's eyes as if she were the engineer of Adoyo's remarks. "I would be dead by now, either I or my children, old as they are," he proceeded with a little relief, his lover responding with nods of assent. "It is my responsibility to uphold cultural laws and practices, made and exercised by our ancestors."

"But," Akuom interrupted, "how is your daughter involved in this case? Please tell me what she said."

"Imagine," said Akondo, "Adoyo told Onyoyo that wife inheritance fuels the spread of HIV!"

The words struck Akuom's spine like thunder. She jerked backward and forward like somebody seated on a springboard.

"What's your take on this?" Akuom asked.

"Most of our people," Akondo said, "die from *chira*."

Akuom smelled danger in going too deep into the issues, given her rich cultural background. She understood that her hard earned, golden relationship was at stake.

The purpose of their remarriage was purely cultural, meant to curtail *chira*-related repercussions that would befall their families. According to them, it was a pity that the young generation was falling prey to the western trends that diffused their cultural values.

The couple had drastically strayed from their intended cultural bond as evidenced by their extra-cultural romantic behaviour that raised eyebrows among their audience like Akuom's habit of visiting Akondo's vacated main house to take a look at his historical photo hanged on the wall. With her palms on her cheeks, she could stand at the centre of the floor admiring Akondo's photo taken in his prime as a police officer manning a gate of what seemed to be a government establishment, judging from a drab writing that ended with the word 'Authorities'.

Clad in short sleeved khaki uniform ironed to peel off the skins of flies that would be tempted to land on the state-funded clothes, the disciplined Akondo stood stiff, strong and alert, a baton firmly held to his right hand. A military cap that crowned his career on the head, face uglied to scare away enemies of his employer - the government, black shoes as bright as midday sunshine and stripped socks reaching up to the knees.

"If only I'd discover this man in this state, we'd battle it out with your mother. I tell you, old age has really damaged a son of a woman!" Akuom once irritated Adoyo by uttering such remarks when she

7

intervened to inquire about her problem with the old man's photo after watching her ogling it for extra ordinarily too long.

Adoyo clicked her tongue and left in a huff, suffering a word deficiency situation, although she felt amused later while digesting the remarks in her brain and started giggling to herself on her way to the stream for a bucket of water.

Akuom made tireless efforts of brushing off termites that threatened to consume the photo and placing it in good position to preserve the family object of historical interest. But…! Demons of jealousy that resided in her soul, she gave wicked glances to a photo hanged next to the photo she admired, a photo of Akondo and Adoyo's mother as a young couple possibly a few years after their marriage. Although dressed in the latest fashion of those days, face donning beckoning beauty with hair plaited in the best style, Akuom still sneered at Akondo's deceased wife claiming she gatecrashed Akondo's soul. Akuom, had done no harm to termites feasting on the distressed photo until Adoyo took the responsibility of fighting the insects by brushing and use of insecticides.

CHAPTER THREE

"Next time I'll pinch your chusband cheeks if you repeat the same," Adoyo warned Apisy. She actually went ahead and pinched Apisy's cheeks to express her anger over the young girl's habit of sitting next to Akondo to exchange gossip. "You look like a starving vulture when you walk on your spindly legs carrying gossip to your granddaddy."

"*Yawa yawa!* Mama help!" Apisy screamed.

"There's her grave! Behind your late dad's house! Go; wake her up to help you…! Girl!" Adoyo whispered harshly to her ears, her right hand pointing the direction of the grave where Apisy's mama had been interred a few years earlier. "There's your food!" she barked, shuddering with bitterness as she pushed a plate of boiled potatoes towards Apisy.

"You either eat or go back to your granddaddy to flood his ears with more gossip: 'Granddaddy, Adoyo said ooh…Adoyo said eeh…Adoyo told so and so ooh… Adoyo said nyooof…nyeef!'" Adoyo muttered as she tried to force bites of boiled potatoes through the lump in her throat.

Apisy shrugged and stormed out, heading to the banana grove behind the kitchen. She propped her chin in her palms to narrate incidents that had stoked fire in her aunt's stomach. At the back of her mind, she was certain that her woes had nothing to do with the death of her parents. Her habits would provoke emotions from any responsible parent or guardian. She gave a wicked grin to a stalk of bananas overhead that seemed to be ready for harvest and smelled glory that ironed out the scowl on her face. She dreamily diverted her concentration with a flashback to exciting past experiences with her peers to swat the outrageous confrontation by her aunt from her mind.

Even though mischievous, anything reminding her of her dead parents always blew toxic gases into her breathing system. She thought of visiting her granddaddy in his *duol*, private hut, but flinched; he could be enjoying his sunset honeymoon with his new lover, all in the name of fulfilling cultural requirements.

Apisy picked up some dry pods from a plant curled round a banana stem, pulverised them between her two palms and extracted the seeds that she used for playing a puzzle on the ground. Rays of the sun sinking behind the mountains towards Usenge beach seemed to be absorbing the dregs of food in her stomach. Her eyes browsed across the sky for alternatives but she found it colourless. She threw her frustrations to the wind and walked back to the kitchen.

The messes in the kitchen placed her in a better position to rebuild her relationship with Adoyo. The open kitchen was a frenzy of chickens tumbling over plates and fighting over boiled sweet potatoes strewn all over the floor, most likely a share that was carelessly left on the plate for either her or the birds if she was not willing to eat them.

Apisy collected the potatoes damaged by beak prints and devoured them without considering the extent chickens go while foraging for food, hence the filth on the same beaks that they had used to peck her potatoes.

She gulped down a big mug of water, swept the kitchen while tidying up everything and destroyed the sticky cobwebs that had littered the kitchen wall for years. She left for the bushes around the home to carry back a heap of firewood that would definitely mellow Adoyo's anger unless she was too inhuman.

"Look here, my niece! Respect me, as you would your parents," Adoyo advised Apisy. "What dream do you have in life?" she asked her.

"I dreamt last night that my late parents, seated in front of our dilapidated house were calling me to go and greet them," Apisy replied, beads of tears rolling down her cheeks.

"*Choke!* Are you being haunted? When I ask about your dream in life I mean your hopes in life! Not those ghosts you see at night! OK?"

"Thank you, aunt. My dream is to drive my car."

"Girl! Will you pick that car from the roadside? I mean what would you like to be when you grow up that will give you the car you dream to own?"

"I'd like to be a nurse."

"Thank you. What must you do to become a nurse?"

"I must work hard in school."

"Good. And what next?"

"I must respect my elders."

"Good girl. I want to help you but I still have more questions for you."

"Yes, Aunt."

"How old were you when Odima, your dad, died?"

"Six years old."

"Good. What about Akungu, your mama?"

"Eight years old."

"What about Okech, your younger brother?"

"Seven years old."

"What about Adogo, your last-born sister?"

"Six years old. She died in the same year as dad."

"How many people were you in the family?"

"Five."

"And how many are alive today?" Apisy's tear banks broke, resulting into a loud cry.

"Please stop crying and answer me. I want to help you!"

"I am the only one left."

"And how old are you now?"

"Twelve years old."

"Consider that and change," Adoyo concluded. Her remarks peeled off a layer of crud from Apisy's behaviour.

Apisy visited the banana grove and lay down on a felled banana stem to digest the questions and remarks from her late dad's youngest sister.

Apisy rued her status as a total orphan and stared helplessly at rays of light peeling through banana leaves that seemed to draw clear lines of her character tracks. Her time for change seemed to be long overdue but she crafted an alternative that would force a drastic turn of events.

At the back of her mind, Akondo's granddaughter knew exactly the right personalities that would help in building her future. By the use of her little finger, she counted: it's God, my class teachers and my guardian, Adoyo.

Even though she cracked jokes and had lots of fun with her granddaddy, Apisy's respect for him faded away day by day due to his sunset honeymoon that had seen him relapse to infantile behaviour. The spectacle of an old couple swinging around the village in the latest fashion reserved for the youth and adolescents was an eyesore to people of moral prestige like Adoyo.

The old Akondo, in his late seventies, looked bewildered in white bermuda shorts and wrinkled nose loaded with sunglasses in the guise of helping his deceased cousin's widow. That old grandma looked odd in her tight jeans miniskirt that kept her weary knees knocking against each other with the thud of unprocessed leather under manufacture. The sound of yowling dogs across the village, too, was a sign of displeasure in the animal kingdom.

CHAPTER FOUR

Adoyo felt motivated and encouraged. The Chief, in his capacity as the government representative, had done his part by inviting an anti-HIV/Aids campaigner to his *baraza*, public gathering, a representative of an organisation staging war against AIDS in the village, but the grumble from the grey-haired audience on the bench adjacent to his seat now seemed to be turning tables down.

A white man who accompanied the campaigner spoke in English language interpreted in Luo by the campaigner. He made it clear that he was only present on the introduction day but would not be available subsequently for field work due to his duties in the office.

The audience loved his accent but some, like Akuom failed to even pronounce his name; Johnstone Smith. Akuom repeatedly mispronounced it as Komsom amid laughter from Apisy and others who understood English. For the sake of peace, Akuom resorted to describing him as that white man who filters English through his nose.

They seemed to express displeasure at the activist's approach to *chira*. His teachings left their thoughts in turmoil. He refuted claims of the existence of *chira* and insisted on a deadly infection that kills if not well managed.

Seated with stoops, the half-interested audience avoided eye contact. They gave wicked glances with a skeptical expression to the son of their land who had a negative approach to the laws made by his ancestors.

Adoyo gritted her teeth but felt encouraged by a section of the congregation, mainly townie faces, who seemed to have no interest in negative cultural practices. But the facilitator, in his wisdom, trimmed his words, carefully balancing between positive and negative cultural practices in consideration to the village folks deeply ingrained in cultural beliefs.

His teaching on origin and purpose of wife inheritance jangled the nerves of cultural doyens like Akondo and his lover Akuom. His revelations proved beyond reasonable doubt that his research expertise elevated him to a higher level than the elders twice the age of his dad.

According to the facilitator, the sanctity of wife inheritance was not solely for sexual gratification. The Luos started wife inheritance on their long voyage from Sudan in pursuit of greener pastures.

According to the custom, men inherited their brothers' widows to provide security and material support but conjugal support was applicable only if the widow was still in her reproductive age and required the latter for continuity.

Akondo's generation had slowly bent the traditional belief to a purely sexual exercise, marred by luxurious episodes, a cultural upheaval that contributed a lot to the spread of AIDS virus. The current generation of lawmakers winnowed out the clause of material support and replaced it with another that promoted the well-being of wife inheritors, putting them in a better position to live luxurious lives while offering the service to a widow.

The culture of pampering wife inheritors, he said, was deeply ingrained in widows. They believed that an inheritor was as delicate as an egg and risked breaking if not well handled. He could exit prematurely before the exercise is complete and, worst of all, reveal sensitive issues about the deceased's family.

The leisure enjoyed by wife inheritors enticed the lazy young blood, who opted for wife inheritance rather than going for the bothersome responsible marriage. They inherited women the age of their mothers, who lured them and used them for the cultural practice and sexual gratification.

Akondo and his beauty had scored higher than most villagers involved in the exercise. Their age difference was below five years,

Akondo being the older one, a challenge to aged widows who fancied messing around with young boys.

Akondo also provided for his lover, contrary to the norm of entertaining inheritors at the expense of family resources.

The session seemed to gain ground as the facilitator delved into negative cultural practices that fuel the spread of AIDS virus. Scowls on faces stiffened harder, mouths pursed, hands on chins. Adoyo and others who abhorred such cultural practices gained morale for further advocacy. Murmurs and grumble inherently went silent.

"Somebody to give us examples of negative cultural practices that fuel the spread of AIDS virus," he continued.

"Yes," he said, pointing at Apisy, whose hand was raised at the back.

"Men who throw stones onto rooftops of huts where girls sleep," she responded. The answer tickled youths in the crowd who chuckled facing the ground, faces covered with palms.

"No, that has nothing to do with culture although we advocate responsible sexual behaviour among youth."

"What do you mean by responsible sexual behaviour?" Akondo asked with a mischievous grin.

"There are three ways: one – abstinence, two - use of condoms and last - being faithful to one sexual partner."

"Elucidate," Akelo's luminous boyfriend shouted from the bench occupied by teenagers.

"Abstinence means staying without having sexual intercourse with anybody until you get a responsible partner whose status is known to you."

"How will you know the status?" he pressed.

"By going for voluntary counseling and testing (VCT) in any health facility," the facilitator answered, then sank his hands into a carton behind his seat.

He pulled out a box of condoms, opened the box and peeled off one condom from the sticky batch. The sight of condoms flapping in the breeze from the tips of the facilitator's fingers revved up assorted reactions from the audience before he opened his mouth to explain and demonstrate how it is used.

While cultural activists viewed it as the peak of rottenness in the society, change agents gave nods of assent to a solution that would help prevent the spread of HIV.

Cultural hardliners stuck to their guns. They insisted that AIDS is a new wave of *chira* resulting from the conduct of the current generation that has failed to live in compliance with the laws made by their ancestors. It called for the intervention of the most experienced medicine men to prescribe charms that have the powers to entangle the wrath of the angry ancestors.

"What do you do if you visit a VCT centre and find yourself positive?" Akelo asked, with a scared look.

The facilitator waved to a female colleague seated next to an assistant chief to stand up and carry on from there.

"I am in the best position to talk about living positive, because I tested positive one decade ago but I am still living, strong and confident," she testified with conviction. She went on to create awareness on the use of HIV medicines.

She taught at length about responsible sexual behaviour, and encouraged good diet that boosts the immune system.

According to her, HIV healthcare providers prescribe medicines depending on the viral load. They subject their clients to viral load tests that provide information on the health status and how well antiretroviral therapy (ART) is controlling the virus. The aim of the therapy is to reduce the viral load to undetectable levels.

"Yes, mama. Do you have anything to share with us?" she acknowledged Akuom's raised hand.

"I am *Josapin* (Josephine) Akuom. My address (husband) is *Parasis* (Francis) Akondo. My only comment to the young generation is to think wisely on their approach to our culture, otherwise we are bound to face the wrath of our ancestors."

A group of teenagers, amused by her old-fashioned pronunciation and way of introduction, burst into laughter.

Adoyo's approach placed her in the best position to lead the facilitator's recruits, hired to spread the awareness creation messages to the grass roots.

CHAPTER FIVE

"But it's a taboo for a girl to repair a roof in her parents' home," Akondo commented sheepishly to Akuom.

Adoyo overheard her dad's complaint expressed in hushed tone as he left through the back entrance behind his main house, flanked by his lover. She ignored him and, using a long stick, continued to toss off lumps of soil that matted the grass.

Wise boyfriends used the crumbly lumps of soil to rouse their girlfriends but mischievous ones threw solid stones, causing tremendous damages to the roof. They dented the roof, leaving the sky clearly visible from inside the kitchen. Rays of light, peeling through the holes when the moon was up, caused nightmares among the beauties who spent their nights in the kitchen, forcing them to seek divine intervention. The situation worsened during rainy seasons when the girls would be forced to huddle at a corner to avoid the intruding showers.

Adoyo had decided to hold the bull by its horns. She mobilised all the ladies who benefited from the kitchen space to join hands in repairing the damaged roof. She sent Apisy on an errand that reeled five girls of the eight beneficiaries from their respective homes to her venue. The beneficiaries responded to her quest with alacrity and gave contributions depending on their capacities.

Apudo, the youthful divorcee, whose dad's farm flourished with ripe roofing grass promised to provide as much grass as was required to do the work. She had spent her nights in the kitchen for the last one year since she dumped her husband with two male children.

She blamed the man for infidelity that had broken their marriage, but who was who? She herself was lousy with boyfriends who caused damage to Akondo's kitchen roof. Worse, she had no reason to beg for a sleeping place outside her parents' homestead. Her mother's kitchen had a bigger space than Akondo's kitchen but she had moved out simply to be free from her father's restrictions.

The second beneficiary was Akumba, a brown short girl who had a network of veins round her arms that looked like wire-mesh. She pledged to influence her younger brother, Omogo, known for his skills in roof thatching, to provide the service free of charge.

Akumba's excuse for failing to sleep in her parents' homestead was that her mother's kitchen roof had been blown off on a gusty evening. The only house in the compound that remained vacant was her late elder brother's hut, but it was a taboo for a daughter from the same family who encounters menstruation to spend nights in it. The other hut belonged to

Omogo, her last born brother, but she couldn't spend there on account of privacy and cultural restrictions. Adoyo refuted her claims and linked her dodging to the vicious dogs in their homestead, trained to crash fishy eyes peeping through the fence to steal her from the hallowed compound after sunset.

The third beneficiary, Akoyo, a brown, slender girl with some two identical mounds of flesh on her calves, did not hesitate to open up and reveal that she was an adult and needed her freedom. She taunted her dad that while he was having fun with his wife, her mother, he expected others to remain stiff like corpses in the morgue.

"Bind him in the name of Jesus!" Adoyo cursed her remarks. She promised to prepare meals for Akumba's brother while he would be on duty.

The fourth beneficiary, Abuogo, a fat, cute bling bling lady who donned two heaps of bangles on both hands, opted for arrogance as a way of self defense against anybody asking her why she never slept in her parents' homestead. She applied the same any time she was asked a question pertaining to her character.

"If you feel I am too fat to sleep in your mama's kitchen, chop off the excesses in my body and allow me to sleep," she once told Adoyo, who had asked her why she decided to walk all the way, across the stream,

24

leaving good houses in her parents' homestead, to pursue courtesy of the poorly constructed and cushy kitchen. Abuogo promised to provide a hen to be slaughtered on the day of the roof repair.

The fifth beneficiary, Achola, whose mama was a dealer in *andiwo*, brew, was notorious for excessive consumption of her mama's products. She'd be messy and reckless after drinking. Her reason for begging to sleep in Akondo's kitchen was understandable because her widowed mama had no capacity to repair the dilapidated kitchen built by her late husband eons earlier. And worse, the mama had the burden of keeping her lazy *jalako*, widow inheritor, who could spend the whole day under their mango tree preening himself and demanding expensive meals. Village psychologists linked Achola's conduct to frustrations and trauma.

Achola's offer to bring a glass of the brew to entertain Akumba's brother was scoffed at by Adoyo, although the rest thought it wise to accept the idea, considering Omogo's addiction to the brew.

Three more beneficiaries whose contributions were essential had not turned up. Apisy, exempted in consideration of her tender age, provoked hostility by saying that her offer would be to taunt twilight boys whenever their stones landed on the grass thatched roof. None had the guts to openly express anger but their facial expressions were a warning sign to the minor.

25

Amami, the sixth beneficiary, a daughter to Akondo's younger brother, the late Rabidhi, whose homestead was adjacent to Akondo's, had left a week earlier to visit her aunt miles away. She had promised to travel back a fortnight later.

The repair would be a smooth ride if the pledges already made were fulfilled. Adoyo was not worried about those who were absent, knowing that they'd definitely be there to spend the night in the kitchen that same day. Akelo had told Apisy that she had gone to fetch water, although it was likely that she and her luminous boyfriend were enjoying the afternoon breeze at a secluded place.

Achando, a willowy figure-eight beauty, was not a liar. Apisy had met her on the way to the village open air market where she had gone to buy some millet for her mama. Achando was the only girl in a family of seven and was a mother to one, a son called Akula. She asserted that being the only girl, she needed to spend her nights in the presence of other ladies.

Ten girls: nine youthful adults and one minor, Apisy, spent in the kitchen. Two members of the family that owned the kitchen; Adoyo and Apisy and eight beneficiaries who begged for the sleeping space for weird reasons.

After telling tales and sharing their day to day life experiences with lovers, a mat donated by Akondo was spread on the floor followed by an old mattress bearing the colour of crude oil for the girls apart from Apisy and her aunt, Adoyo who had a different mattress for themselves. The hosts had requested beneficiaries of the sleeping place to bring with them mattresses and blankets but things seemed not to be working possibly due to protests from their parents who were against the habit of sleeping away from their parental homes. The old mattress and blanket used by the girls had been inherited by Akumba from her deceased elder brother.

***

"Your big eyes! Throw it here!" Omogo quipped at his helper from atop Akondo's kitchen roof. The boy on the ground tied the grass in small thatches and threw them to Omogo up there.

Omogo applied his skills to repair the roof. He held the bottom parts of the thatches in a firm grip, twined them left and right with the intelligence of an experienced roof thatcher. Then he laid them carefully over the holes that had been bored by the stones thrown there by the illicit lovers.

With a mischievous grin, he gushed out obscenities that cracked the ribs of his elder sister and her company.

"Get out of here! You sinner's bell," he shouted, tossing off a stone with his toe.

The beauties who were busy preparing meals as they monitored the work progress tried their best to ignore their young brother's foul mouth.

"Leave him alone, he must have visited your mama before reporting here," Achando whispered to Achola, whose hackles had started rising. She felt like throwing a stone at him.

"By the way, where is our old man and his 'baby girl'?" Achando turned to Adoyo's side and asked. Adoyo scowled at the way her friend described that old woman who had robbed her of her dad.

"They've gone for a stroll," she responded in a light tone, her fractured temper under control.

"Did he have any issues concerning what we're doing?" Achando asked, twisting her fingers as a sign language to explain the gist of her question.

"Which issues?"

"Like *chira* or something of the sort?''

"I didn't ask him," Adoyo shuddered. Achando sensed that she had to stop asking more questions of such types.

Adoyo's friends had learnt to comply with her dos and don'ts. As much as she respected her culture, she abhorred negative cultural practices, especially sex oriented ones. This was a time when the wind of a deadly sexually transmitted infection was blowing across the globe.

People of high morals believed that if they failed to adhere to such practices, they'd face the wrath of their ancestors. But what kind of wrath was this that went beyond the *chira*-infested Nyakonja village?

Akondo accorded his last-born, unmarried daughter the respect she deserved. He could only gossip about her but avoided confrontations, considering her character that earned her moral accolades.

Adoyo did a forward march and pinched Apisy's buttocks from behind. She had watched her for quite too long. Tickled by Omogo's remarks, she shouted praises and encouraged him to yell more taunts at the beauties gathered together to see their sleeping place renovated.

Omogo's brazen remarks were primitive and retrogressive, but his clients swallowed them hard and avoided rubbing shoulders with him to gain from his knack for rural crafts. His presence was a boon to the community. His services were hired for as low as a bottle of *andiwo*. He had no dependants and accepted even a few coins he was given for his services. His older rivals in the same profession envied his offers that robbed them of clients.

Omogo sulked for a few seconds over Adoyo's action. He then decided to rejuvenate Apisy.

"Apisy, Pis Pis!" he called, but the crying Apisy declined his call.

"Apisy, Pis Pis!" he called again.

"Yes, Omogo," the teary Apisy responded.

"Please give me a mug of drinking water," he requested.

"Not you! Who sent you?" Omogo snarled at Achando who had made a step forward to bring the water. She seemed not to have understood Omogo's intention.

***

Dazzled by the new look of the kitchen roof that pumped a fresh breath of life to tired souls, the girls rejoiced together.

They jabbered joyfully as Omogo descended from the roof using a wooden ladder. They sang praises to Adoyo for her brave decision to do the work against all odds.

To conclude his work, Omogo trimmed off the grass hanging below the edge of the roof using a wooden board and a panga. Akondo's kitchen now looked livelier than his main house, whose rusty iron sheet roof reflected his age.

Akondo's departure from this house to operate from his *duol* after inheriting somebody's widow had reduced the value of the house. It had degenerated into a mere breeding place for rats and bats attracted by weevil infested cereals stored inside. A taboo restricting him from spending with an inherited woman in his late wife's house evacuated him

30

to his *duol*. He believed that Adoyo's mother was actively watching from somewhere in the spirit world. He risked getting *chira* if he was tempted to do the forbidden.

Although the cultural laws allow the wife inheritor to sleep in the same bed used by the widow and her late husband, an inheritor who happens to be a widower is barred from doing the same. But Akondo occasionally spent nights in the bed used by Akuom and her late husband. They operated in shifting modes, spending a night at Akondo's home in his *duol* and the next night at Akuom's home in the house they had shared with her late husband.

Gossip and blame-game dominated the meal relished by the frenzied team celebrating the successful repair of Akondo's kitchen roof.

"Attention, my fellow women!" said Akelo. "We thank Omogo for the good job he has done today but I request you to tame your boyfriends to curb the stone throwing habit that damaged our roof."

Akelo's plea provoked a storm of protests from her colleagues. It was like a notorious thief advising people to stop stealing. They rebuked and reprimanded her for talking as if she herself was innocent. Apudo asked her to state clearly before them if a stone had never been thrown onto that roof on her account.

31

"When?'' the agitated lady retorted. "When was that and who was he?"

"The luminous one," Apisy muttered to herself, coyly looking down, her eyes focused on the plate of chicken soup placed on her laps.

Achando burst into a silly chuckle, covering her mouth with her right palm.

"What have you said?'' Akelo roared. "Tell me what you've just said, young girl, or I'll pinch you harder than Adoyo did!"

Gales of laughter erupted in the group. Apudo, seated on the green grass next to Omogo's high table, coiled herself to the ground, holding her ribs with the left hand to curb stitches caused by excessive laughter.

"Tell them!" Omogo yelled from his high table where he was busy peeling flesh from the drumstick and chewing. "Tell them, Apisy! Pis Pis, tell them!"

***

Akondo sat with his lover in front of his *duol*, exchanging whispers and cheeky giggles as they admired the repaired roof of his kitchen, which now sparkled in the bright moonlight. He felt thrilled despite his qualms with Adoyo's action.

Unperturbed by the rumours spreading around the village of what had transpired in his homestead, which had irked staunch disciples of culture, Akondo felt an irresistible urge to thank his daughter.

"But-but-but thank you….daughter!" he stammered.

Adoyo ignored her dad's cowardly voice echoing through the eaves of her late mother's dilapidated house.

She had made a U-turn after spotting the weary knees of the aged couple halfway exposed to the moonlight, a kink that interrupted her attempt to go for a short call in the groves behind her dad's homestead.

Akondo had stayed away from his home to extricate himself from the ignominy of confrontations and taunts from cultural law breakers and law makers. His agemates would definitely urge him to stop the new development while at the back of his mind, he was certain the spirited youths, who had no more respect for him, would laugh him off. He spent the day enjoying a happy moment with Akuom at her late husband's home.

9pm local time, Akondo's kitchen was as lively as if it was daytime. The excited maidens were still listening to stories from Amami on how life was in Yimbo, where she had gone to visit her aunt. She spoke about the girl hunters over there, and the community's approach to the deadly wind that had left the society in a confused state, whether it was *chira* or HIV.

Amami freely told stories of death cases and the circumstances surrounding them. "On Saturday last week,'' she narrated, "I attended the burial of my buddy, who had been ailing for quite sometime; the paper doctor had diagnosed her as HIV-positive and having throat cancer—"

"But what caused her death, according to you?" Adoyo cut her short.

"According to me, the girl made love to a boyfriend before her widowed mother got an inheritor."

"Serious!" the tipsy Achola exclaimed, threat etched across her face. "That was a *chira*!"

"And'' Achando cut in, "do they have a common sleeping place where girls from all over the village spend, to share experiences?"

"They wish they had. Their homesteads are scattered far apart though, you see. The land is bushy and lousy with wild beasts that attack people at night, making it impossible to walk to a sleeping place away from your home. Even boys who walk around the villages looking for girls at night must be well armed to reach their girlfriends."

"Amami,'' said Abuogo, "tell us about their alarm system. Do they also throw stones to alert their girlfriends?"

"No, the boys are trained to whistle. They uniquely twist their tongues with skills that can only be understood by their girlfriends; any other fool will assume he's a drunkard wobbling on his way back home."

Amami's audience burst into loud laughter, except Adoyo, who was aware that the story had reminded the audience about her dad's whistling skills that outsmarted the young boys' retrogressive stone throwing habits. He was the only lover known for whistling to his '*baby girl'*, as they fondly referred to her, in unique styles that nobody in the village could mimic.

Apisy, who could not control her joy, made it worse by shouting out loudly: "Parasiiiiis!"

This new name of Adoyo's father was gaining popularity in the village. The village replica of Romeo and Juliet was the aged couple.

"What about their accent and dialect?" Akoyo asked.

"They speak with longer vowels that sound more attractive than ours, with slight variations in use of words like the word *jalako*, to them is *jater,* to mean wife inheritor or widow inheritor. They used to laugh a lot as they listened to my stories because my language, to them sounds like another language altogether, or Dholuo, yes, but a funny or distorted one," Amami answered.

CHAPTER SIX

Akondo and Akuom walked in style, entering the compound of Achola's mother, who was busy attending to her ailing inheritor. The inheritor's condition caused tremendous losses to Akuota. Her clients even though consoled her as they consumed the illicit brew, they spread lots of exaggerated lies about circumstances surrounding his health condition.

Akuota, Achola's mother, accorded her visitors the respect they deserved being aware that the couple rarely visited other people unless there was a special reason. In this case, it certainly was about the inheritor's illness, for Akondo and Akuom were not consumers of her products.

Akuom entered without struggle, but Akondo's American height forced him to bow while entering Akuota's bedroom to avoid knocking his head on the wooden frame at the top part of the door.

Ogoma, the notorious inheritor who had served more than twenty widows without pitfalls, lay on the bed staring at the roof in a manner likely to suggest that he was pleading with his ancestors.

"Let's pray," Akuom requested wearily. She prayed:

"Almighty father who looks at us from His hideout in the spirit world! The father of our ancestors! Obong'o Were! Listen to the cry from a daughter of your creation. I know I am not clean before you, King of kings. I belong to the mankind that is weak and filthy with the sins of this world, Creator of Heaven and Earth! But when we turn to you for sympathy, Oh God of Heaven and Earth, kindly forgive us and listen to our plea, God of miracles. Ogoma is your son, brought to this home by your sympathetic hands to save the seeds of Akuota's womb. Kindly take control of angry ancestors who are fighting her husband from the spirit world, oh God! Ogoma is an innocent saviour who deserves no wrath, Almighty! I pray trusting and believing in Jesus name! Amen!"

Akuota's failure to fend off her clients from the sitting room where they were busy sipping *andiwo* would plunge her into more troubles. As much as they pretended to close their eyes in honour of Akuom's prayers, they were busy taking audit of every word she used in pleading with Ogoma's creator.

Akondo lifted the blanket that covered Ogoma's body and moved his right ear closer to the patient's face for some brotherly conversation, done in hushed tones, both for privacy and in regard to his condition that could not allow him to speak loudly.

Ogoma complained about persistent backache that intensified when he tried to sleep on his right or left side and a strong headache that pulsated in the veins of his neck, making it hot, as if water was boiling in his throat.

"The saviour bit more than he could swallow!" a drunkard, seated on a chair in Akuota's sitting room, shouted as he vanished in the shrubs behind her home.

"Take heart, my brother," Akondo encouraged. "My brother, Rabidhi, Amami's deceased father, suffered from the same condition."

"But did he recover?" another drunkard, seated near the door with a glass of *andiwo*, shouted and fled before Akondo could finish his words of encouragement.

"Lower your tone please. These eavesdropping drunkards are killing the spirit of my husband," Akuota pleaded.

Reactions from drunkards who took advantage of Ogoma's condition to ridicule his lover were a clear reflection of the feelings of the clients, who hid their hatred when Ogoma was well. They had ill feelings about the privileges he enjoyed while other men were working hard to make ends meet.

He used to enjoy copious amounts of free alcohol. His meals were prepared with the best culinary skills ever. In fact at times, Akuota sought expertise advice from experienced cooks, just for Ogoma's sake.

Rumours spread around the village that Ogoma was an enemy not only to men who missed the same opportunity but even to chickens, because all their eggs were fried for Ogoma to appease his spirits. They'd cackle whenever they saw him, running around the compound and flapping their wings as if they had gone mad.

Akuota's only cow was not spared either. Ogoma could sulk and refuse to take tea if it did not have the right amount of milk. With the little sciences he learnt in school, he knew well how to calculate the ratio of milk to water in a cup of tea. Ten molecules of milk plus one molecule of water could serve Ogoma well but if the widow made a mistake of mixing say seven molecules of milk to one molecule of water, Ogoma could splash the offer onto the table and leave in a huff. The cow grew thin and weak due to excessive milking that left its calf with nothing to suck.

Odhialo's two biological children, Achola and Ombwede, hated Ogoma to the bottoms of their hearts, considering him to be the devil in their home, a leech. Ombwede, the younger brother to Achola, could spend a better part of his day running errands meant to fetch goodies to entice the stranger he was being forced to call his dad. Terrible!

Akuota always reprimanded her son for giving Ogoma wicked glances whenever the inheritor addressed him as, "My boy or my son".

Unlike the late Odhialo, who could toil in the family farm for a whole day, Ogoma spent his day under a mango tree, in its cool shade, behind Akuota's house. There he would preen his beard and admire his face in a broken mirror always kept in a pouch that he had snatched from Akuota. He made Akuota his dustbin of emotions and mood-swings.

Akuota's *andiwo* business was not her wish. She engaged in it as a result of the bread winner's death. Handling drunken clients was the worst of nightmares she went through.

Ogoma's condition caused disquiet among cultural crusaders, who sought various ideas to save the practitioner who had fallen ill in his line of duty. Desperate for any alternative that could offer solutions, Akuota heeded advice and warnings from all sources, some illicit.

Naive herbal activists, mostly her clients who had never been in the field, pontified about herbal solutions by taking her round the fence, pointing at the leaves of various plants they claimed to have herbal solutions. This actually, they did for the sake of winning a glass of her products. Others whispered to her ears in hushed tones, calling names of people suspected to have bewitched her.

Ogoma's legitimate family kept off his woes. Akwede, his wife and the mother of his five biological children, did her daily chores as usual without regrets. As one of the few individuals in the village who were convinced that AIDS is real, she kept off her husband due to his reckless sexual behaviour. His children also could not put up with the reality that their father was the best service provider in the wife inheritance fraternity.

Akwede had severally defied negative customary laws as proof that she was a staunch believer in the modern civilisation. Her decision to build a new house in the home she and her husband shared, and to stay in it without involving him for some sex oriented cleansing rituals according to culture, was frowned upon by society.

Her action had pushed Ogoma to the edge. Contrary to his belief that the wife would one time plead with him to take her through some cultural rites that a woman cannot do without her husband, she did the unexpected. She barred Ogoma from spending in the house that had actually been launched in his absence.

Cultural experts had warned him against spending nights in the house, regarding underlying consequences - *chira*.

Although considered a loss to Ogoma, it was a boon to widows looking for inheritors. Ogoma kept on shifting from one widow to another to help them fulfill their cultural needs. They secretly thanked Akwede for 'donating' her husband to them.

CHAPTER SEVEN

"Straight on the floor, stretch your legs! Put your palms on the floor to support your body as you look up the roof!" the witchdoctor ordered the half-naked Akuota, only left with the ragged skirt to cover the bottom part of her body.

He shook her chest like somebody shaking a gourd of sour milk being prepared for consumption. The folds of skin on her flabby belly vibrated simultaneously as she danced to the tune of her doctor's commands.

Akuota endured all this to achieve her goal for the day; otherwise, she would count losses. She had offered her bull for the exercise, and had walked all the way to the doctor's place, miles away from her home.

She sincerely found herself in an unfamiliar situation, this being her first time to visit a witchdoctor on her own. She had last visited a witchdoctor in the company of her mother, as a little child.

The doctor's shrine was not conducive for human life or any living thing depending on oxygen. His sooty grass thatched roof was a haven for bats and vectors. The wall was coated with a black layer of soot that seemed to have taken years to form. The floor was damaged with holes dug by the gymnastics of clients during treatment.

The bushy vegetation of huge sacred trees and shrubs required the intervention of authorities responsible for controlling human-wildlife conflict. The shrine had neither a fencing system nor human settlement around.

Akuota trembled with fear as her doctor growled, twitching the pupils of his eyes weirdly, with his head facing the roof. The pungent smell emanating from his body clearly indicated the wedge between his spirits and the bathroom.

A hulk of a man, seated on a small round traditional chair with a circumference that accommodated only a small fraction of his massive butts.

"Odhi..! Odhi..! Odhialoloooo..!" The name forced its way out of the doctor's mouth as he trembled, his body vibrating as if he was dancing a jive. He shook Akuota, making her wish to escape, but the surrounding seemed to have been cordoned by some powerful spiritual forces. She gritted her teeth and hung on.

He jingled the beads cascading down from the strings tied round his feet and hands. Solution was underway, as long as she could endure the weird treatment process. Her worst fear was seeing the face of her late husband if the doctor's charms brought him down from the spirit world.

The doctor heaved his chest and breathed out like a deflating balloon. "This war is more than I expected!" he opened his eyes and grouched. "Did you go through the cleansing rituals after burying your husband, before accepting an inheritor?" the doctor asked with a scowl on his face. Akuota cleared her throat but suffered a word deficiency syndrome.

"Please tell me the truth for us to get the best remedy."

"I don't know those rules," Akuota whimpered.

"Who's Odhialo?" the doctor asked.

"He's my deceased husband."

"His spirits are hovering above the roof of your house, reeling with anger, for you wished him a quick death. You intended to break the chains of marital restrictions so as to mess up with worthless loafers who move from one widow to another, sowing their wild oats. My sister, inheritors are required to sail you through the rituals that all widows go through after burying their husbands, but...! It is an affront to your husband's supremacy to allow a man to sleep on his bed, before a single leaf of any plant grows on his grave, before the tears of mourners dry up, before the dust of death that killed him is blown back to the sea, before he packs his luggage to travel to his ancestors' final residence, there he sees a man giddy with excitement, engaging his wife! My sister, it is a sign of you

44

celebrating the death of your man!" Akuota became fidgety on her seat as the doctor gave this sermon.

"My affinity to the ancestral spirits will enable me to win this battle but it is tougher than I expected," the doctor whined.

He sidled towards a range of gourds on a dark corner of the hut, tapping them one after the other with his index finger like a scientist testing the acidity of liquids in a number of test tubes. He finished with a gesture suggesting that he didn't succeed in his mission.

He scratched his bushy chin for a moment and started afresh. His finger got stuck to one of the gourds as if it had some magnetic force. He trembled with vigour, gyrating violently round and round, shaking the gourd and singing queer songs addressing Odhialo and other powerful famous ancient names known to have sowed seeds that brought the clan into existence.

The proceedings had already deluded Akuota into believing that she had landed on the right soil, contrary to her earlier fear when she had based her judgment on the grotesque image of the doctor and his bushy shrine.

When he calmed down, he turned to his pots arched round the edge of his wooden bed and remoulded his style, this time round sinking his index finger into the herbal concoctions and dripping this onto his tongue.

45

"Jah...! jaaah...! jah....!jah....!" the doctor barked, shaking his head with a repulsive reaction to prove to Akuota that her case was not a joke.

Akuota's face crinkled up with disgust as she stayed put to listen to the next voice from the spirit world.

"These are grievous seeds of disaster, sown by our people!" the doctor pronounced. He clicked his tongue and turned round to face his client.

"My sister, your enemies are more than I expected. Who is this Akwede I see shedding tears in the mirror of my pot?"

"She is the legitimate wife to my inheritor."

"When did he last provide for them?"

"I don't know." Beads of sweat formed on Akuota's forehead.

"Some divine forces sympathising with the family of your inheritor have joined Odhialo's spirits in the war against your family. They won't kill you outright, but will torment you by sending bouts of diseases that will keep you and your inheritor writhing in pain until you adhere to their demands. But relax; I know how to go about it. Did you carry the sample of soil from your husband's grave?"

"Yes," she said, delivering the soil wrapped in a polythene paper. The medicine man moulded the soil using herbal concoctions from one of the pots and gave it back to her with instructions on how to bite and swallow. He instructed Akuota to stand up on her two feet and do some

46

continuous high jumps repeatedly, saying from the bottom of her heart: "Odhialo, my husband, I beg for your sympathy. The monkey on your throne has conceded defeat; he's appealing for your sympathy!

Akwede, my sister, I know I am a snatcher of the pillar of your home. Please forgive me!"

The stick used by the medicine man to stir some magic solution on a pot was not for fun but to test the seriousness in her heart as she gushed out the words. He stirred the liquid with glances flickering between Akuota's face and the pot.

The forty-six-year-old widow found the assignment more taxing than the labour pain she had gone through while delivering Ombwede.

The physical exercise she was required to undertake was really demanding. It was, to her, a reminder of her school days as a sports girl, but this time round she was forcing into action the cackling joints of her body, worn out by age and health complications.

Another challenge was uttering words which she would not utter under normal circumstances. How would she refer to Ogoma, of all the people, as 'the monkey' when all along she had been showering him with endearments: food for my soul, pillar of my house, husband of widows, father of orphans and all beautiful praises you can imagine? Having to

47

plead with her competitor and, worse, refer to her as *'my sister'*, would subvert her pride and ego.

Akuota, together with other beneficiaries of Akwede's conflicts with Ogoma, always yelled taunts at Ogoma's wife, referring to her as a careless woman who did not know how to take good care of her husband.

She had no business with Ogoma, the golden jewel any woman would strip naked to save from a snatcher. A widow once told her in public that she was like a beast living in a sugarcane plantation but unaware how juicy the plant is.

Akuota's body was flooded with sweat as she made several attempts to heed the medicine man's order, each time failing the test. She proved to the healer that she was physically fit but spiritually, the medicine man had to allow nature to take its course and look for other alternatives.

The doctor conjured some gimlet eyes and looked at Akuota curiously from toe to head.

"Is it possible for you to spend three days away from your home for this mission to get accomplished?" he asked.

"I fear for the health of that inheritor I left in my house. My daughter is stiff-necked and cannot take good care of him."

"The man talking to you is the one in control of those spirits pursuing his life."

"I have no problem as long as you gag them."

"Fine, I'll host you in my main home for those days as I prepare the best charms that you'll carry back home."

"Thank you."

A short distance away from the doctor's facility shrouded in thick bushy vegetation was the doctor's residential home. Scared by the brooding silence in the forest, Akuota made huge fast steps, cringing away from the giant trees stooping and swaying gently overhead in the waning moonlight. Dancing shadows of gangling trees swaying from side to side in the night breeze sweeping through the forest. The blood curdling quiet forest saturated with divine powers multiplied in size, making it difficult for Akuota to reach the open. The steps she made forward seemed to be taking her backwards. She became squeamish and screamed at any slight movement on the grass beside the shrouded footpath on which she was walking.

The open space unveiled a big traditional Luo homestead, awash with grass thatched huts. A stout muscular man battling with the weight of logs of wood used for closing the gate downed his log to usher in the new client.

"Welcome my dear. Are you from the doctor?" the man asked cordially.

"Yes, sir," Akuota answered.

"OK, my name is Oura. Feel welcomed. Follow me to the visitors' house."

Akuota sat in the commodious visitors' house, impressed by the hospitality of her doctor and his family. Although mud walled, it had an iron sheets roof and a number of rooms to provide enough space for visitors' accommodation.

Akuota felt groggy after slogging away for a whole day at the doctor's hostile health facility. She felt relieved, at least breathing fresher air than the smoggy one at the doctor's shrine.

A gigantic woman dangling a pair of long pendulous breasts joined Akuota in the parlour reserved for chatting, resting and open discussions. She plonked herself on a seat across the table after a word of greetings and introduced herself as the first wife of the doctor.

They exchanged civilities and she moved to the next business of taking Akuota to the room Akuota would use during her sojourn.

She led the client to where she would take a bath, a small area fenced with thick vegetation. Akuota enjoyed the bath of warm water served in a water trough.

When she returned to her rest room, she found a bowl of steaming boiled chicken and a plate of ugali placed on the table. Odhialo's widow felt her strength and courage restored. Her confidence in the doctor's service soared.

8am the following day, when Akuota woke up, the doctor was still nowhere to be seen within the compound. Akuota remained calm and optimistic, hoping the medicine man was busy in his secluded shrine, preparing solutions for the war she was facing back home.

Three more women introduced themselves to the client as the second, third and fourth wives of the doctor. They lived in the same compound. Only the first wife seemed to be the age of her husband; the rest were as young as his daughters and ran up and down the compound doing domestic chores.

Akuota felt it was normal. She understood witchdoctors' ability to confuse young maidens and draw them into their vortex of love. Trying to seduce a witchdoctor's wife was a seed of disaster that could damage a man's life forever. Rejecting his romantic advances could also affect a girl's pursuit for the right suitor.

The doctor's home was a residence for more than thirty dependants, some of whom had no blood relationship with him. They claimed that even after their successful treatment, some ancestral spirits living in the bushes surrounding the doctor's shrine held them back there.

One of the doctor's daughters, who paid frequent visits to Akuota for a chat in the sitting room, revealed to her that the man who had ushered her in upon her arrival was a man whose origin was not known. He had visited the doctor as a nude mad man two years earlier but stayed put even after getting treatment. He served in the home for no pay. He would turn wild any time he was told about his origin. He referred to the medicine man as dad and did the donkey job that even paid employees would not do.

With their rich background in traditional healing, the doctor's dependants kept his clients busy by teaching them on cultural practices and messes that would sow seeds of disaster to grandchildren of Ramogi.

In her consultation with the doctor's wife concerning cleansing rituals to be done by a widow before accepting an inheritor, the doctor's first wife gave her step-by-step instructions:

✓ As soon as his soul leaves the body, spruce up the body before alerting the public, and lay it in the open, like his sitting room, on a mat, and cover it well.

✓ Get out into the open and scream loudly to arouse the public to mourning.

✓Take his spear, if he had one, and run to and fro the nearest stream, pointing in the air as if you want to kill. This chases away bad spirits of death.

✓After burial, allow an elderly woman who has performed all the cultural rites to shave your head, leaving not even a single piece of hair. Never have this done by a naïve young woman who still has many stages in life to go through, for her life would be at risk.

✓Wash your body in a stream or river away from where people go to fetch water to drain the spirits of death.

✓Don't enter somebody's home or go to public places while you still have 'okola', the status of a person who has just lost a spouse and not yet done with the cleansing rituals in accordance with culture. The spirits of your deceased husband may harm the people you meet.

✓Wear his trousers for a number of days to feel his presence in your body until you're certain his spirits are settled in the planet of his ancestors.

✓A year or so after your man is settled in the spirit world, get a man of your capacity. If you own a home, don't kill somebody's son by accepting a boy still living in his parents' home; you'll harm his future marital development. Neither should you accept a bachelor; he's not recognised by our ancestors.

The woman's teaching tasted sweet like honey. Akuota wished she had met the doctor's wife before the death of her husband; she wouldn't be carrying the burden on her back. She was relieved on the part of the man's age which was not touched on by the advisor. Ogoma was five years her junior.

Akuota looked down upon the flamboyant, youthful wives of the witchdoctor even though they wangled some advice from their elder co-wife's teachings. The teachings were flimsy and insincere. The doctor and his first wife were aware of the challenge and kept the clients in closed door meetings when such advisory sessions were in progress. They heeded the doctor's warning against interfering with the elderly doyen of culture who had contributed a lot to the development of their shrine.

The medicine man's young wives randomised teachings as they heard them from the doctor and his first wife and used them to seek publicity by wangling their way into the clients' rooms in the absence of his first wife and exercising their skills. Occasionaly they would gather leaves from different plants to prepare herbal solutions and put them to test. The first wife was in the best position to inherit her husband's health plant due to her ability to sustain it.

"If a man beats you, chew this," one of the younger wives told Akuota, handing over a bunch of leaves to her.

"If your co-wife bewitches you, boil this and use the solution for bathing," another one seated in the middle said, handing over another bunch to Akuota.

"If a woman snatches your husband, lick this," the third one, seated at the end, advised Akuota, handing her some ash wrapped in a polythene paper.

Their cheeky giggle as they performed the health service was clear proof of the irrelevance of their participation. Akuota handled them with the instinct of a mother. They were agemates of Achola. She declined their request to divulge details of her problems that had forced her to visit the doctor.

"I just came to visit the doctor but I've no serious issues," she answered the one seated in the middle.

Their first children were crawling babies of the same age. It was as if the doctor sent his charms forth for three beauties meant for marriage in the same year. Akuota realised the difference when the first wife locked them out while offering her service.

Akuota trembled with fear as she watched three service men, one of them Oura, struggling to contain a mad man and pushing him towards the clients' house. The new client, who had just been attended to by the doctor, was extraordinarily energetic and violent. He hurled nasty insults

55

at his handlers and unleashed free for all blows anyhow. He seemed to have a powerful allergy for clothes and bathroom. His hair was shaggy, eyes protuberant and bloodshot. His body was oily, stinky and produced prodigious amounts of sweat. His jigger-infested feet were crooked and shapeless.

The doctor's three teenage wives huddled together at a secluded place near the fence, whispering taunts and looking at him with some silly grins.

Overcome with fear as they approached the entrance, Akuota fled through the exit door and took refuge in the fenced bath-place behind the house. They locked him in a room next to Akuota's but he broke the door open and engaged them in a fist fight that left Oura spitting blood.

The sentence that he repeatedly uttered, with a pained expression on his face, gave a clue as to the cause of his madness: "Apondi! Apondi! I long-long to see you! Apondi! Apondi! I long-long to see you!"

His sister, who had mobilised energetic community members to bring him to the doctor, was there to answer questions pertaining to Apondi and how the name swirled around his mouth like whirlwind. His community members who had brought him here were sent away for the sake of privacy. Once they handed him over to the doctor's trusted service men, they had left but his sister had been forced to stay within to handle intimate details of the patient.

She was the right person to speak on behalf of the mad man who hardly uttered any word other than the name 'Apondi' and remarks expressive of a desperate situation.

"Come over please," the doctor's first wife who rushed to secure Akuota beckoned.

"I am afraid the mad man will kill me," she moaned.

"Just come over; I'll be with you throughout," the doctor's wife appealed.

Akuota sat next to the doctor's wife under a mango tree away from the clients' house, listening to her explanation as to why the patient was still hostile after visiting the doctor.

"He's still busy preparing herbal solutions that you'll carry home with you tomorrow. He normally doesn't attend to a second client before he's through with the first one, which can rattle the spiritual forces concerned. Otherwise, the man would now be very calm," she explained. "Those men will be there throughout the night for your security."

"Have you done anything to establish the roots of the name he calls continuously?" Akuota asked, relieved.

"Yes. His sister has just told me it's the name of his divorced wife from Alego. The woman used the powerful Alego charms to bewitch him. Are you aware that the most powerful charms come from Alego?"

"Yes,"Akuota responded with a smile, "they say Alego is called *the roof of magic.*"

Akuota's last night in the traditional patients' ward was a sleepless one with a thrilling live movie. The mad man fought his handlers the whole night without rest. The men applied all the skills they had in the boxing fray but he felled them all.

Banished to a corner of the sitting room, the safest distance for watching, Akuota enjoyed the drama that attracted all the people who lived in the doctor's compound together.

Apart from the doctor's elderly wife, the room was jammed with fans cheering the new boxing champion who had joined them on that day.

Applause from the fans seemed to be oiling the joints of his fists to do an even better job. The incident was declared a crisis at around midnight when the three service men yowled in pain, pleading for back-up. Four of the doctor's teenage sons joined the men with a new approach. They brought in some sisal ropes normally used for tethering cows, tied up his hands together at his back, did the same to his feet and laid him on the floor. He entertained his fans for the rest of the night by singing good songs he and Apondi used to enjoy together during their honeymoon.

On Akuota's last day in the doctor's home, her healer had not arrived by ten o'clock in the morning. She felt home sick. She was worried about her clients, left under the care of her arrogant daughter.

She expected a jumbled mish-mash of bad reports from her clients and the balm for her soul, Ogoma. The mad man had since succumbed to a deep slumber, putting the drama to a pause.

The ancient looking traditional healer sauntering from the gate with a basket of herbs relieved Akuota of her worries. The doctor's first wife directed Akuota to a hut whose purpose she had not known for the days she was there. She learnt after entering that it was the exit house, where clients were cleared just before departure.

The doctor joined Achola's mama in the hut, closed the door behind him and sat on a traditional three-legged chair, facing her.

"Thank you for your patience, my sister. I do handle cases as gruesome as the mad man you shared the house with. Don't be surprised if you meet the same man some day later talking nicely to you. Let's finalise this business today, hoping all will be well."

The doctor pulled out a bunch of fresh leaves from his basket and handed it over to her.

"Take it with you. Chew a leaf together with your man. Boil the rest and wash your body with the herbal solution," he instructed.

"Thank you, sir," Akuota appreciated.

He pulled out some powdery mixture of pulverised dry leaves mixed with ash and wrapped it up in a polythene bag.

"Lick this everyday together with your man after supper," he instructed.

He sank his hand into the basket and pulled out a piece of bone.

"This bone is from a pig; let it dangle from a string tied round your waist. Whenever you meet Ogoma's wife, turn it to her direction. Make sure it is well shrouded beneath your dress; it loses power any time it meets the eye of a person apart from the man who inherited you. Don't be cajoled into believing that any pig-bone has the same powers, this special one is empowered by my charms," the doctor instructed and warned.

He pulled out another polythene bag containing some black powdery mixture of unknown origin.

"Sprinkle this to the food prepared for your children but don't let them know. It's a secret affair between you and your man," he instructed and warned.

He pulled out a spangled waxy shell which must have been extracted from some sea reptile, perhaps a turtle. Akuota could not identify exactly the animal that had lost its life to save Odhialo's family.

"Clasp this in your armpit any time you go for an errand outside your home; it'll protect you against husband snatchers," he instructed.

The doctor folded his basket and placed it aside. He cleared his throat and looked straight into the eyes of Akuota.

"Listen to me. As you leave here, strictly follow these rules:

✓ Avoid any contact with the shadow of a fig tree until you're through with the dosage I've administered to you – apart from the pig-bone and the shell which you'll use for the rest of your life.

✓ Avoid eye contact with Ogoma's legitimate wife; she'll steal some powers from you.

✓ If the first person you meet when a day breaks is a woman, go back home and start the journey afresh until you meet a man; that'll determine your fate for the day.

✓ Whenever you have a nightmare about your late husband, go out in the middle of the night and kick his grave with your right toe and spit on it twice. Don't divulge that to your inheritor; it may harm him.

✓ Whenever you differ with your inheritor over any issue, go to an anthill at midnight and sit on it for two hours without swallowing a single gulp of saliva. If by mistake you do, repeat the whole process until it is successful.

✓If you differ with children sired by your late legitimate husband, go out at night when the moon is up and look straight at the moon for two hours without blinking. If by mistake you blink even once, you have to repeat the whole process from the start. If it happens when the moon is down, revisit me for a solution.

The doctor concluded his instruction with a word of thanks. He lifted his hands for a word of prayer and released Odhialo's widow.

CHAPTER EIGHT

Akuota looked behind and saw the doctor's health facility nestling in a shroud of thick forest across the stream. She heaved a sigh of relief, feeling some burden had been lifted off her chest by the healer who had held her hostage for three working days. She counted the benefits she had registered after offering her bull in exchange for the witchdoctor's services.

The basket packed with herbal medications wrapped in a shawl contained the remedy for the negative forces fighting her family back home.

The distance back home was almost a three miles walk but that was a smaller task compared to the day she trekked to the doctor's place, loaded with the burden of disasters from seeds she had sown herself.

She broke into a trot with an aim of reaching home before sunset. She felt home-sick and worried about Ogoma, but had confidence in Akuom, who had promised to look after him in her absence. The two widows sailing in the same boat did a lot to support each other, just like Akondo did to support Ogoma, although Akondo envied Ogoma for the influence that enabled him to inherit a bigger number of widows than he himself had done, the power that had seen him named *The Choice of Widows.*

For heaven's sake, Akuota had no business harming anybody's life, not even rivals such as the other widows in the same village who yearned for the same man. She never used any magic to sustain Ogoma for that long, just competent hospitality and love which oiled the ligaments of a man.

Other widows who lost the village hunk to Akuota cited several messes which they blamed on her. For example, her neighbour Akoko kept on shouting barrages of insults at Ogoma the whole day, worst of all telling him that he had failed to provide for his legitimate family.

Ogoma had left Akoko prematurely before performing all the rituals, and crossed the fence to Akuota's home, just a few weeks after the burial of Odhialo.

Throughout Akuota's conversation with the medicine man, she had never asked him to bewitch any of her competitors, but only to cure Ogoma, her ailing inheritor. If at all she had intended to, the first culprit would have been Akoko, who always hurled insults at her across the fence, calling her all sorts of names; husband snatcher, *andiwo* seller, night-runner, transmitter of *sihoho*, and all dirty stuff you can imagine.

Akuota avoided the main road and weaved her way through foot paths and tracks in the bushes to dodge nosy pedestrians concerned with issues that had nothing to do with them. She walked through dormant tracks shrouded in grass and desperate for users. She rubbed shoulders with wildlife but pressed on.

"Jesus!" Akuota slammed on the brakes that flung her body onto the thorny shrubs beside the path she was thudding. The huge leafy tree casting shadow in front of her was a fig tree!

"Thank God for saving my life!" she mumbled to herself. She was just inches from her grave when she realised it. Her right foot was about to thud the soil covered by the shade of the fig tree. She sprang up after thanking her god and diverted by jumping over leaves outside the circumference of the shade then resumed her walk on the path.

Human population in Nyakonja village had built structures all over places. The bushes had been cleared for agricultural purposes, denying wildlife and implicated people, like Akuota here, an opportunity to hide. She stood stranded in a sugarcane plantation near a stream that delineated the boundaries between Nyakonja and its neighbouring village. Any attempt to go ahead would expose her to unwelcome scrutiny.

Akuota remained calm in the warm glow of the setting sun, waiting for darkness to envelope the village and cover her in her final steps back home. The scary sound of fighting mongooses ousted her from the hiding place.

Two hours after sunset, her heart was still pounding from fear of eleventh hour traders who could be on their way home from the market, but why? Everybody was in hurry at that moment and nobody could bother her about the contents of her basket! Just too suspicious, she was.

Like a mother rushing home either to prepare supper or to open the kitchen for her chickens, Akuota lolloped, occasionally jogging even, to get to her destination.

"Akuota of the Ogoma's and Odhialooo's!" shouted one inebriated man in a group of drunkards staggering on the wayside near the path leading to her home.

She sped off to avoid getting into any form of conversation with them. They had missed her and could go as far as trying to inquire what the basket contained if she had made a mistake of responding to their calls.

"Your daughter is a devil! She thinks this world belongs to her!" another one shouted, prompting her to inquire on what had transpired between Achola and her clients while she was away.

"*Choke!* What's wrong with you?" a woman she knocked down accidentally on the sharp corner near the back entrance of her home whined. She only realised after saying sorry that the victim was Akoko, the village noise maker who also looked drunk at that moment.

Akuota's decision to avoid the main gate and use the back entrance was wise. She'd be clearly visible hence subjecting herself to public embarrassment, mostly from her clients who were probably in the house swigging their brew.

Silence engulfed Odhialo's compound. Ombwede's *simba*, personal hut, was closed, rays of light filtering through the slits of the door made of reeds.

Akuom's voice whispering to Ogoma in the bedroom buoyed Akuota with the spirit of victory.

"Aku...Akuom!" Akuota called in a guarded tone, knocking the bedroom window.

"Thank you, my sister! Welcome, welcome back please!"

Akuom rejoiced, prying the door open. They hugged, exchanging words of encouragement.

Akuota hurriedly entered the bedroom and met Akondo's face before moving to her soulmate, whose physical appearance was also promising.

"Thank you, my brother, for taking your time! Oh God! What a wonderful thing to have people who can sacrifice in turbulent times!" Akuota rejoiced, hugging Akondo.

"Greet him and listen to his voice," Akondo urged, propelling Akuota towards her inheritor.

The couple intertwined their hands round one another and remained in a fixed position, clutching each other in a word deficiency situation, but just moaning. She was shocked to find her man in a sitting position, which had not been possible at the time she had left for the medicine man's place.

"Let's go to the sitting room for some discussions, the space there is wider," Ogoma suggested as he sprang out of bed.

"I was cautious because I thought I'd find drunkards making noise here," Akuota said, sitting on the sofa bought by Odhialo before his death.

Akuom joined Akuota on the same seat on one side while Akondo and Ogoma sat on the side next to the bedroom door traditionally meant to be used by the owner of the house.

"Your daughter did wonders on the day you left," Akuom reported.

"What happened?" Akuota asked with a curious look on her face.

"She got drunk on the *andiwo* you left for sale and exchanged blows with a client," Akuom cracked her ribs with laughter as she reported.

Akuota clicked her tongue, suffering a word deficiency syndrome.

"Any other problem while I was away?" she inquired.

"Your cow chased our dear man, Ogoma when he went for a short call, almost goring him but he ducked." Akuota's heart missed two subsequent beats and resumed with a force that shook her body like an earthquake.

"If it were not for milk it produces, that's the cow I wanted to take to my doctor. He knows well how to gag bad spirits," Akuota expressed her grief.

Akuota had no fear to divulge details of her experience with the medicine man to this couple. These two were the ones who had introduced her to the traditional healer.

"I am finally back. The journey was good. He gave me all I need to protect my home," Akuota revealed.

"But just keep them with you and use them as instructed. Don't divulge them to anybody! Not even to me," Akondo instructed.

"He also told me the same," Akuota said.

"Another development that happened while you were away is the coming of the door-to-door HIV/Aids activist. He involved Ogoma in some closed-door counseling and testing and advised him to go to Kaluo Health Centre for HIV drugs.

"I've no problem as long as they don't stop us from using the herbs given to me by the traditional healer," Akuota responded with ease.

"Generally, what's your comment about the medicine man?" Akondo asked.

"That man is ambiguous. He's a healer with his own natural powers. A medicine man of great eminence, armed with a variety of herbal solutions that cure even mad men. He's generally good," Akuota praised.

"No problem. I know you have a lot to explain to Ogoma as per the doctor's instructions; kindly allow us to leave," Akondo requested.

"Thank you, dear ones," Akuota appreciated, opening the door to release the frail couple.

Akuota moved her chair closer to Ogoma, placed the basket right in front of him and started:

"This, is a pig-bone, empowered with the charms of our doctor to protect our relationship against jealous people. It'll hang from a string tied round my waist, shrouded beneath my dress," she explained.

"When?" Ogoma asked.

"Right away. Any delays will make us vulnerable to danger."

Akuota rose from her seat and made two steps towards the bedroom. She groped for a string in the dark room and pulled out one from a heap of tattered clothes that had been re-purposed into a pillow.

She returned to her seat and tied several knots that failed to tie up. Ogoma intervened by applying Odhialo's rusty drill from a tool box stored behind a cockroach infested cupboard in the sitting room. Akuota warned him at finger point, against any attempt to drill the magic bone. The underlying consequences would be dire. Any particle that made up the bone had its own powers; hence drilling would turn a portion of the bone into an empty hole.

Ogoma used his rope-weaving skills to net the bone in its own pouch of interwoven sisal rope. He tied one end of the rope to the bone and advised Akuota to drape it around her waist with the other end tied with a loose knot.

"Thank you," Akuota appreciated with a sigh of relief.

"This is a shell from an unknown creature, most likely from the sea, the bedrock of our ancestral spirits. He advised me to clasp it in my armpit; it'll also protect me against some bad forces," Akuota cleverly avoided revealing to Ogoma its main purpose, lest it made him too proud and more finicky in his demands for services.

"This powder is for my children. I'll sprinkle it on their food like salt, but it remains a secret affair. They're not supposed to know," Akuota said, placing the polythene bag of charms on the floor in front of her man.

"These leaves are ours," she said. "You and I chew a leaf; it strengthens the bond between us. We boil the rest and use the herbal solution for bathing." Ogoma beamed at her.

"These are pulverised dry leaves mixed with magic ash,'' Akuota continued. "We'll be licking it everyday after supper; just you and I."

"Thank you,'' appreciated Ogoma. "Did he have any grudge with the paper doctors who move around telling people about AIDS?" he inquired.

"No, throughout the treatment process, he never told me anything against them."

"The AIDS awareness creation activist was here while you were away."

"Tell me all about him."

"He came with a test kit and diagnosed me as HIV positive."

Akuota flushed and shook slightly but steadied herself and regained composure.

"Did he do it publicly or privately?" Akuota inquired, shock written all over her face.

"No, it was a closed-door counseling and testing," Ogoma responded gently.

"Did he give you any drugs or any solution?" Akuota inquired.

"Yes, these are HIV drugs. He referred me to Kaluo Health Centre from where the drugs were administered to me," Ogoma explained.

"For how long will you use the drugs?" Akuota asked.

"For as long as I live. They don't cure, they're immune boosters."

"Don't cure...?"

"No, they don't cure. AIDS is not curable, but HIV drugs help us to live longer," Ogoma explained, with the wisdom of a victim who had undergone some counseling.

"What else did he tell you?" Akuota advanced her concern.

"He told me that you're also supposed to go for the same test to enable them to handle our case as a couple, and not just I as an individual."

Akuota shook slightly, with no immediate reaction against the report.

A state of confusion descended upon the couple for some minutes. They wondered whether to follow the paper doctor or the traditional way.

They resorted to using both; after all, none had advised against another. They jointly chewed the leaf prescribed by the traditional doctor, licked the powdery mixture and moved to the next step. Ogoma reclined in the sofa as his soulmate boiled the solution in a traditional pot.

***.

Akuota behaved like a hired crook to anybody trying to glean information pertaining to her disappearance for some three days. It had left her clients exposed to mistreatment by her reckless daughter.

She felt freer when at home either serving clients or doing domestic chores, relieved of the burden of clasping the magic shell to her armpit but errands out of her homestead exposed her to the torturous task of locking her left armpit, the holder of the magic shell that forced her to stick her left arm to her chest, a gesture that made her look like a victim of stroke.

She braved her way into repairing the dilapidated kitchen to provide space for culinary activities and, certainly, for her daughter. The ongoing medical services, with details confined to her bedroom, required maximum privacy and security.

She arranged some three stones at a corner of the bedroom to serve as the fireplace conveniently for warming the herbal solution every night before use. She improvised a curtain out of her green bedsheet and hanged it on the bedroom door to curtail advances of hawk-eyed, nosy clients with other interests besides their drinking leisure.

"What kind of food is this that tastes like boiled cowdung?" Achola squealed, chucking her plate of boiled *omena*, fingerlings, onto the floor.

"What is it, daughter?" Akuota ran to the kitchen in response to her daughter's distressed reaction.

"Mama! Why do you like serving us dreck from the dustbin of your man?" Achola snorted.

"Sorry, Apisy visited me this morning and volunteered to help me in washing the plates but it's like she didn't rinse them well," Akuota used the young girl as her shield.

She understood and said in a soft tone: "OK, but I won't eat that food."

Achola's reedy voice sparked reactions from her only brother, who entered the kitchen and politely placed his plate of the same food on the floor. His departure without a word provoked Akuota's plea for understanding.

"Kindly come back, son," she pleaded with Ombwede who was flailing his hands towards his hut which stood solely on the right-hand-side of the home near the fence, in accordance with the custom.

"Kindly wash those plates afresh and serve the *omena* left in that cooking pot," Akuota requested her only daughter.

"Pus… Pus!" Achola called their cat that had already devoured her share splashed onto the floor. She served it Ombwede's rejected share. She sipped a mouthful of water, swilled her mouth out, washed the plates and served her brother and herself, this time round enjoying an odourless, delicious meal. They had initially been served contaminated stuff with a nauseating smell and insipid taste.

Akuota hurriedly reached out to Apisy to appease her by donating an exercise book after tarnishing her reputation. The cheeky minor would otherwise spread some bad gossip about her.

Akuota knew exactly the magic substance that had contaminated her children's food but had to defend herself against mistrust from Odhialo's orphans.

Akuota proceeded to Akondo's *duol* to consult with them on how to apply the substance to her children's food without harm. She told him about her bad experience while trying out the witchdoctor's stuff.

"Imagine, I had to use your granddaughter as my scapegoat," she confessed.

"Don't sprinkle magic powder on your children's food as if it is salt; just a very tiny amount on the tip of your finger," advised Akondo.

"Remember, magic powers have nothing to do with amount. Spiritual forces will detect their presence even if you apply the smallest unit of the stuff."

Akuom turned left to face Akondo, whose ribs were cracking with laughter punctuated by choking coughs.

"What a naïve girl. Always contact us in case you have any challenge," Akondo encouraged.

Akuota left the house fighting back the grin on her face. She was impressed at having caught the couple unaware in a compromising position. They were spoon-feeding each other on a plate of rice and discussing matters of importance when she entered. She regretted her lack of courtesy to knock before entering Akondo's *duol*.

***

Akuota took her seat to attend to her clients, who started trickling in on getting wind of her presence. It was like opening a whole new can of worms after staying for quite sometime without rubbing shoulders with that drunken trash.

She unveiled a jerrycan of the grog brewed to the required standards. She distributed glasses to the clients and served the brew according to their orders using a portion of a plastic container cut to the size christened *ondago*, their version of a pint, which contained ten shillings worth of the brew.

The man on the seat next to the couch facing her was a renowned mason nicknamed *Okebe*, moneyed, Onyoyo's eldest son. He could place an order enough for all the clients to drink themselves silly. The creases on his forehead were tingled with sympathy as he watched the poor addicts giving their petty orders from the peanuts they earned from menial jobs.

Like a Good Samaritan filled with the spirit of giving Akuota a big welcome back to her business, he sipped a paltry two *ondagos* of the brew while waiting for the number of clients to swell. Akuota hopefully served buyers with a repulsive response to those who wanted the brew on credit, notorious borrowers who hardly paid.

Twenty-seven customers were twice the number Akuota's house could accommodate. Others, therefore, had to use the benches outside her house.

She sidled towards the flamboyant buyer who had beckoned her for his big offer: "Count the number and serve each of them five *ondagos*, then give me the bill."

"Twenty-seven times fifty equals one thousand, three hundred and fifty shillings," Akuota whispered to him.

"Take this and bring me the balance," the building contractor said, handing over two thousand shillings to Akuota.

"God bless you," Akuota appreciated with a smile. She stomached stingy remarks from customers, gushed out in parables as they sang praises to Okebe.

"A very generous and hardworking man, Okebe! Who can compare you to lazy wife inheritors wandering from home to home to suck the blood of widows?"

"Long live Okebe. Your development record is miles away from idle wife inheritors who spend whole days preening their beards in shades as they wait for food prepared by poor widows of our village."

Inured to the inherent behaviour of drunkards, Akuota focused on the benefits of their presence rather than venting out her anger at whatever they said. She did not wish to bite the hands that fed her.

From the seat he occupied behind Akuota's house in the scorching midday heat, thawing out his body after a long sleep in the bedroom, Ogoma randomised the insults targeting him. Over the time, he had developed a thick skin against such sharp remarks.

"What would you do if somebody came to your home to inherit your mother and sits there the whole day without doing anything productive?" a young drunkard whose widowed mother had snubbed inheritors for a decade after his dad's death asked his friend who was an agemate of his.

"I'd slice off his nose and ears," the friend answered without hesitation.

The drunken yobbos dawdled over their drinks after gulping down Okebe's offer. Akuota's meekly response called for a reconciliatory approach to mend the fences; otherwise, they risked losing sympathy next time they visited her in the absence of Okebe. They aired their grievances as a way of mending fences with Akuota.

"Akuota, while you were away, Achola hit me with an uppercut to my chin and chopped off a huge chunk of flesh using her long nails," a client complained.

"Akuota, while you were away, Achola splashed a glass full of hot *andiwo* on my face and kicked me out of your house."

"Akuota, while you were away, Omogo ridiculed Ogoma by telling him he looked like one of the monkeys jumping up and down your fence." Akuota smiled at the report that reminded her of the order to describe Ogoma at the witchdoctor's shrine as "the monkey".

The mortified *andiwo* vendor deliberately declined their plea. Okebe, who had remained silent all along followed Akuota to her house for a swap of civilities and proceeded to Ogoma's resting place behind the house.

They cracked jokes and reminisced about their childhood, learning together as primary school kids.

The crowd of drunkards staggered away in different directions, feeling the pain of their own tongues stinging back at them. For heaven's sake, Okebe had no grudge against anybody. His offer had just been out of a good heart, contrary to their assumption that he was inciting them against Ogoma. He and Ogoma shared lots of childhood experiences, which bound them in a relationship too strong to be broken by the wealth of this world.

"Carbon dioxiiiiiide! CO_2!" the sound of a drunkard from across the stream, rippling through the vegetation to Okebe's ears provoked him into action. His childhood nickname with an origin too demeaning to expose to the public was being quoted.

Okebe sprang to his feet and lolloped towards the stream to establish the source of the sound. Okong'o, a former schoolmate of his, who had been two classes behind him, stood on a dead anthill across the stream, trumpeting his shameful childhood name after consuming the drink Okebe himself had offered. Okebe felt like elongating his arm to cover Okong'o's mouth with his palm.

He stood there, angrily staring at the drunkard who vanished in the shrubs after realising he was being watched.

Okebe felt that his world had crumbled down if that's what somebody could do to him after benefitting from his generosity.

A fight of drunkards a short distance away from Akuota's homestead mellowed Okebe's anger. He joined Omogo in cheering them as they exchanged weak, crooked blows and blames on who had been the first to speak in parables targeting Ogoma.

***

Okebe's beer-belly wobbled beneath his massive pair of breasts as he trotted forward to catch up with Okong'o who was sprinting desperately for his dear life.

"Today you'll know me!" he threatened, lolloping forward behind his target, his little piggy eyes red with anger.

Okong'o's light weight propelled him faster than his opponent whose body was overloaded with fats from expensive meals he consumed daily.

Okong'o started hyperventilating. His pursuer was still determined to get him. "Forgive me brother! It was alcohol influence, my master, please forgive me!" he pleaded.

Okong'o's appeal for forgiveness fell on deaf ears. Omogo, delighted at the scene, was making the situation worse. He ran behind the village tycoon adding salt to the wound. "If you forgive him,'' he said to Okebe, "he'll be worse next time! Remember, somebody calling you carbon dioxide! You're too clean to produce any whiff of that bad gas, Okebe! Don't forgive him! It's too demeaning to refer to you as CO_2 with all the respect you deserve in this village. Don't forgive him!"

Omogo's low-tone incitement as he jogged behind Okebe kept the fire burning.

"*Wuuwi!* Okebe what's wrong with you? Don't you have the courtesy to listen to your brother's plea?" a crippled woman weeding vegetables in a farm adjacent to the path screamed to Okebe.

But Omogo quickly dashed Okong'o's hope. "Go ahead'' he said, "and deal with him! Don't listen to that crippled transmitter of *sihoho*."

Okong'o succumbed to a sprain in his ankle near the village spring-well, giving Okebe an opportunity to pounce on him with kicks and blows.

"Beat him! Punch his nose! Kick his mouth! He has defamed you, Okebe; kick his buttocks!" Omogo joyfully jumped up and down celebrating the fight as Okong'o yowled in pain pleading for sympathy.

"I am suffering from chest pain, brother. Forgive me…ayaye mama! I have sprained my ankle, brother! Forgive me! I was drunk, my brother! Forgive me…ayaye mama!"

Thrilled by Okong'o's cowardly plea, Omogo danced joyfully, yelling taunts at the loud-mouthed societal leech.

A bunch of beauties jabbering on their way to the stream plonked down their water buckets to rush to the scene on hearing Okong'o's yowl which had degenerated into a groan. The maidens wailed in sympathy for Okong'o, who lay on the ground with a damaged mouth smudged with blood. They yelled words of blame at Okebe for his lack of sympathy towards a man who had conceded defeat long before the fight started.

The fight that ensued at a secluded bushy place with no spectators to separate them saw the winner exploit his potential to the last bit until Okong'o's nose started spewing out plumes of grave gases. Akumba, who happened to be in the group, warned her brother in tears against involving

83

himself in such gruesome activities lest he sowed seeds of disaster that would haunt him for the rest of his life.

The noise made by the group of girls attracted more people from around the village, who scoffed at Okebe for being so inhuman. Akumba rushed to the stream for a bucket of water, to be used for the first aid. The first aid was done jointly by the rescue team.

"Can you tell us what happened, please," Akumba asked Okong'o following a public demand to reconcile the two before the crowd dispersed.

"OK, Okebe offered to buy alcohol that made us drunk and disorderly," Okong'o said. His shaky voice seemed to be hiding something crucial.

"Tell people what happened between you and Okebe! Don't hide behind alcohol! Why couldn't he fight the entire group of drunkards who enjoyed his offer?" Omogo ordered, Okebe looking on with a killer face.

"OK, I went out of control and started shouting Okebe's bad childhood nickname," Okong'o shivered from his latest experience as a result of using the name in question.

"Tell us the name!" Achola ordered.

"Carbo…carbo…carbon dioxide!"

A heavy load hung on Okong'o's lips as he struggled to pronounce the name that had provoked Okebe into action.

A group of men held Okebe tight to stop him from unleashing more blows. He stood still and stiff, huffing and puffing, body drenched in sweat, soul bleeding, sparks of anger flaring all over his face.

The girls laughed heartily. Their laughter grew louder as soon as they moved away from Okebe's earshot.

"Let's talk about the elephant from a safer distance," the tipsy Achola suggested to the ladies carrying buckets of water on their heads uphill towards Akondo's home.

"OK, Okebe is almost eight years older than me, but I know well how the nick-name came about," Apudo, the divorcee in her early thirties, and the eldest in the group, offered to explain. "He's the man who spoilt me with love when I was in Class Six," she said, her remarks sparking fresh laughter from her colleagues.

"OK, go ahead," Achando urged.

"I first heard the name from his classmates, who had christened him Carbon dioxide because of his careless farting habits either in class or outside whenever pupils were involved in a joint school activity. They taunted him with the name Carbon dioxide or CO_2.''

The girls who had been mere babies during Okebe's days in school listened with interest.

"Did you also smell or hear the fart erupting from his trousers or it's just hearsays?" Amami asked.

"I confirmed that when I started dating him," Apudo proceeded.

Water splashed from the buckets on the heads of the girls onto their chests as they giggled at Apudo's revelations.

"How? How did you confirm?" Abuogo gleaned.

"His blankets smelled like rotten eggs."

The girls jointly chorused the notorious *fwan*, a women's laughter that is only applied when a secret, mostly touching on someone's private life, was revealed: *"A heeeeeee..! Auh!"*

"Like, how old were you by then?" the demure Adoyo asked.

"Just a year older than Apisy."

"Jesus!" Adoyo exclaimed while the others reverberated with their *fwan*, *"Aheeeeeeeh..! Auh!"*

"And how old were you when you got married to a different man?" Achando asked.

"Around twenty-two," Apudo answered.

"To be sincere," Akelo said, "Okong'o went overboard if at all Apudo's revelations are anything to go by. With all the wealth that he has acquired over the time and the respect awarded him, calling him with a name that links him to careless farting is too demeaning. Okebe could have killed Okong'o had we not rushed there in good time to save his life.''

"But the beating has caused grievous harm to his already deteriorating health," Achando said sympathetically.

"Why?" Adoyo asked.

"He has been defaulting on the use of his ARVs."

Unlike Apudo's, Achando's revelation suffocated her audience. Everybody gawped at her with scowls on their faces.

***

Okebe shambled along the path leading to Akuota's den in the company of Okong'o. They chatted happily in the warm glow of the setting sun. He was not the type to go boozing around the village during working hours, but in the evening or during weekends.

The crowd of customers seated on the benches outside Akuota's main house stared in amazement at the two cronies who, only a week earlier, were chasing each other and exchanging insults, kicks and blows. Some mediator somewhere must have done a good job.

While the rest gave them a warm welcome, Omogo shook Okong'o's hand with a miserable sneer and twisted his face backwards towards Akuota's kitchen.

Okebe's way of handling issues elevated diplomacy to some level. Tongues were trained to trim words before gushing them out. Nobody so far had said anything bad targeting either Ogoma or Okebe. Okebe didn't mince his words when he threatened to discipline an offender. The man seated next to him, who had accompanied him on his way in could testify on that.

"Give the two of us five *ondagos* each," Okebe ordered, pointing at Okong'o and himself. It was not in order to join people on a drinking spree and start offering drinks without knowing their interests. One could be mistaken to be flaunting his wealth to the poor.

"Somebody to offer me one *ondago*, I'm too broke today," Okebe requested, his voice full of sarcasm.

"Give him on my bill! Give him on my bill! Give him on my bill!" He received offers of more than ten *ondagos*. Some were from those notorious for drinking on credit, whose names featured in the list of bad debtors.

Akuota served Okebe in respect of five serious buyers, avoiding the customers known for visiting the drinking den without a coin in their pockets just to beg from generous clients.

Okebe paid for an 800ml bottle of the grog and placed it on the table to be shared out freely without limitations or discrimination.

"Gulp it down and order for another one!" he yelled.

The jabbering grew louder as the number of bottles going back empty increased. The conduit for gossip could not allow such a big offer to go without somebody being discussed, although this was to be done carefully to avoid stepping on Okebe's toes.

"What happened? I saw Apudo yesterday walking with her five-year-old son sired by her divorced husband," said Ratila, a forty-year-old man rumoured to be a *piti-piti* man, night-runner. This opened a new chapter.

Achola, seated in front of her mama's kitchen away from the crowd, with a glass half full of *andiwo*, observed from behind, concentrating on Okebe's reaction to discussions about his self-proclaimed childhood girlfriend.

"The boy came to visit his mama a week ago but fell sick. They went to visit Achwiya, the elderly woman who knows how to treat *sihoho*," a woman on the bench answered.

"Was he cured?" Ratila asked.

"Yes, the doctor extracted shards of bottles from his stomach," the woman answered.

"Which bottles? Were they beer bottles or soda bottles?" Omogo asked with a mischievous grin.

"You're too naïve!" the woman retorted.

"Omogo, you should know where to apply jokes and when to be serious," Akuota reprimanded amid raucous laughter from the crowd.

"I am not joking. All I want is to stop the child from taking alcohol at that tender age, if the shards extracted were from beer bottles," Omogo said, forcing a scowl on his face to look more serious.

"OK, allow me to explain to you how *sihoho* is acquired to help inexperienced people like Omogo who'll have children in future," the tipsy woman requested.

"Go ahead!" Omogo encouraged her.

"*Sihoho* is cast by evil eyes of witches to their target victims. The magic moves from the eyes of the witch to the victim's stomach, like electric current, and inflicts stomachache that may even kill if not well attended to. Amulets issued by witchdoctors help a lot to ward off evil eyes," the woman explained.

"Another seed of disaster to children is involving yourself in extramarital affairs and touching your child with the filth from your illicit romantic activities," Akuota added.

"What do you mean by filth?" Okebe asked.

"I mean making love to a girlfriend or boyfriend and touching your child before bathing," Akuota elaborated.

"How does it affect the child?" Achola shouted from her seat.

"It may kill the child if not treated," Akuota advised.

"How do you treat that?" Okong'o asked.

"You take the child to a traditional medicine man for an antidote," Akuota advised.

Okebe, unaware of what Apudo had revealed to her colleagues about him, failed to express any reactions to discussions focusing on his self-proclaimed former girlfriend. Furthermore, who knows whether Apudo was just fixing a story to link herself to the village tycoon?

At least Akuota had an opportunity to enjoy healthy discussion from her clients who were notorious for their rowdiness and incidents of fighting whenever they gathered at her place for the brew. She imposed a ban on use of her main house as the haven for drunkards and arranged benches in the open to serve them. Ogoma, who had been warned by his HIV/Aids counselor against alcohol, avoided the crowd.

CHAPTER NINE

Apisy's teacher of English was so aggressive. He taught them how to write a poem in Class Six.

"What did you learn today?" asked Adoyo, who normally perused her books every evening.

"We learnt how to write a poem," she answered.

"Did you write one?" Adoyo asked.

"Yes."

"OK, let me see," Adoyo ordered.

Apisy shared the poem, entitled 'Jalako for Hire'.

JALAKO FOR HIRE

The sweetheart of widows. They fight and sulk, at each other in a scramble, for the love of the man, jalako for hire.

The golden jewel, of widows in the village, they pay to bewitch, to kill and to destroy, competitors for the man, jalako for hire.

He sits in the shade, lazy and idle, waiting for meals, prepared by the widow, jalako for hire.

Chicken is fried, tea is thick, rich in milk, he enjoys on the table, jalako for hire.

He preens his beards, looks at his face, in the widow's mirror, jalako for hire.

He walks in the suit and the shoes, left behind by the husband, of the widow he inherited, jalako for hire.

He pretends to cry, when a man dies, but laughs in his heart, thanks his god, for opening a window, for him to inherit, a widow of the dead, jalako for hire.

He moves to the front, whispers to the widow, don't cry loudly, for the loss of your man, I'm here to fill, the gap he has left, jalako for hire.

His children are dirty, they walk in tatters, his wife is hungry, she goes without food, he belches loudly, his stomach full, of food from the widow, jalako for hire

He leaves in a hurry, dumps the first widow, runs to another widow, whose man has died, she needs an inheritor, jalako for hire.

Adoyo burst into a loud laughter that drew attention of her dad and his beauty, who expressed their concern in whispers. She patted Apisy on the back for the job well done. For the first time, she engaged her in a jovial conversation.

"This is a nice doggerel. How did this come to your mind?" Adoyo asked.

"Our teacher told us to write about anything we know, something facing us in life," Apisy answered.

"OK, keep it up," she encouraged.

Adoyo's prolonged laughter provoked inquiries from her colleagues who had come for their sleep apart from Achola who had relocated to her mama's kitchen after repair, together with Amami.

"Please, tell us why you keep on laughing and looking admiringly at Apisy," Apudo insisted.

"OK, just swear you'll not yell about it," Adoyo warned with a sly smile.

"It's OK, we'll not yell," Apudo promised.

"I want you to read Apisy's poem," Adoyo offered.

94

The girls reneged on their promise to maintain silence and yelled at Apisy with a skein of questions on why she chose the title and how she managed to come up with such serious contents about wife inheritors. They particularly praised the quality of her English which seemed to be higher than her level of education.

Apisy's poem elevated her to another level in the social regard. Her seniors viewed her in a different perspective and drastically changed their approach to her, unlike earlier on, when they could whack her left and right. They realised that her brain was well packed with secrets of people. Probably she would write something about their stone throwing boyfriends next time if given an assignment.

"Even Achola and Amami will be impressed by such a creative writing by our young girl," Achando commented.

"Can we share it with her tomorrow?" Apudo asked.

"Tomorrow is too late," Akumba reacted. "The moon is up and time isn't bad, we can go together now."

"Weeeh…! Ratila!" Abuogo warned in a guarded tone at fingerpoint without expounding details of the name she had just called and reasons as to why she called the name. Everybody knew and indeed shrank a little in fear.

"We're many. He can't face us if we walk together as a team," Akoyo encouraged confidently.

"Let's go!" Adoyo ordered and walked out to lead the team to Akuota's home.

***

Piti-piti… bup! Piti-piti…bup!
The girls scampered to different directions at the heavy sound of footsteps—piti-piti, which ended with a thud – bup, from the compound of a nursery school adjacent to the path they were treading on. The sound of loaded breath - Uuh, which concluded every thud was a sign of a spirited wizard in action in the school compound that had no human presence at the odd hour of the day. He'd make two steps forward, then a long jump that landed him on the ground with the thud - bup!

Apisy lost contact with the exercise book she had at hand and fled towards the stream, screaming cowardly for help from any living thing around. Propelled by the night-runner's powers that engulfed her via a wireless network, she dashed into the stream and waded across to a direction leading to an unknown destination, penetrating shrubs and bushes that dislodged her to Akoko's maize farm from where she could navigate her way back to Akondo's homestead across the stream. Going alone was risky, Ratila had spread his spirits allover places.

She made her way to a nearby homestead that had two grass thatched houses exhibiting human presence. The crippled woman who had intervened to save Okong'o from Okebe's jaws sometime back emerged from the smaller house where she was busy preparing late supper, sniffling and straining from the effects of smoke that saturated the kitchen.

The woman turned right and limped towards Apisy with curiosity at the sight of the minor, ridiculously scared and pleading for help.

"Where are you from at this time, girl?" she asked.

Two adolescent boys, alerted by her question emerged from the bigger house and joined her, equally shocked by the girl's presence in their compound at such an odd hour, far away from her home.

"It is…Ra-ra-ratila chasing me!" Apisy trembled while forcing words out of her mouth.

"Gosh! Ksss! Stop! Don't call his name!" the woman shushed her at fingerpoint.

The naïve Apisy had never known the risk of calling a night-runner by his name that would attract more penalties from the suspect.

"Say night-runner instead, OK?" the woman advised.

"Yes."

"OK, what did he do to you?" the woman asked.

"We were walking on our way to Akuota's home when we heard commotions from the compound of the nursery school across the stream. I decided to run but I could feel some powerful forces pinching my body allover, no matter how fast I ran," Apisy narrated, tears rolling down her cheeks.

"*Choke!* How many people were you?" the woman asked.

"All the girls who sleep in our kitchen," Apisy answered.

"Come in, girl. Come in please," the woman welcomed Apisy to her kitchen. The boys, her sons, equally scared remained outside still clicking their tongues in shock.

"That man is dangerous. He was rehearsing his lunatics before going places to bewitch people, on roads and in homesteads," the woman explained. "Come and sit near the fireplace to warm and dry your body. We'll escort you to your home after supper."

Ratila's powers had indeed drained the food from Apisy's stomach out into the air. She needed to join the hosts on their table for a second round of supper because she had taken supper back home before sharing out her poem.

Apisy felt safe under the care of two adolescent boys, armed with pangas as if the weapons were anything against Ratila's satanic forces.

They crossed the stream using the locally made wooden foot bridge and walked to Akondo's home.

The old man who had been authoritatively ordering the girls not to sleep in his kitchen until they brought back Apisy welcomed the boys to his home ceremoniously:

"Eheheheeeh! My boys! From where did you get her?" Akondo asked, laughing loudly.

"She came running to our home," one of the boys answered.

"Thanks a lot for your sacrifice. I thought the *piti-piti* man had bewitched her to death, I would give several lashes of *okwajo*, walking stick, to all the girls who sleep in this kitchen."

"Are they your wives?" Akuom, standing behind him with a cigarette clasped to her lips, the burning end dangerously inside her mouth, asked mischievously in a low gentle tone.

The girls initially scared about Apisy's disappearance welcomed her back with ululations and praises. Apisy asked them about her exercise book and Adoyo who had picked it from where she threw it while fleeing returned it to her.

Word about Apisy's poem reached the gawky Achola's ears the following day. Her attempt to use Apisy as the weapon against Ogoma failed upon learning that the young girl was too agile to use her feet for measuring the depth of a river.

"Take this to Ogoma, he's good in grammar. He'll help you in making some corrections," Achola advised.

Ogoma too got wind of the poem but it failed to penetrate his bullet proof chest.

The first page of Apisy's book had a funny list of abbreviations:

1. HIV-Human Immunodeficiency Virus
2. AIDS-Acquired Immune Deficiency Syndrome
3. ARV-Antiretroviral
4. VIP1-Very Important Person
5. VIP2-Very Ignorant Person
6. VUP-Very Useless Person
7. MC-Master of Ceremonies

The ladies changed their stand on a message scribbled on the outside mud wall of Akondo's vacated house: OKONG'O IS ON HIV DRUGS. The first suspect in the offensive habit of exposing people's secrets was Achando due to her comment after the fight between Okong'o and Okebe revealing that Okong'o was on HIV drugs. The ladies linked Apisy's poem to some mischief that could drive her to write such an offensive revelation on the wall.

Readers of the message condemned whoever was responsible for revealing such a sensitive issue about a person at a time AIDS had been declared a national disaster to those who believed that its AIDS and not *chira,* but for believers in *chira*, they cursed the author of the message for cheating people that Okong'o was HIV positive instead of telling people that he was a victim of *chira.*

"Whether it's Achando or Apisy, we bind the demon in the name of Jesus!" they cursed.

CHAPTER TEN

Akuota became Akondo's student on matters, culture. The warnings and teachings she received from the medicine man prompted her to develop some relationships with cultural doyens like Akondo and Akuom. She feared for Ombwede's life after her sister's son spent the night in Ombwede's house with a girlfriend ahead of the house owner. Ombwede and his first cousin, a visitor had accompanied Omogo to a village disco when the latter convinced Ombwede to go and spend at Omogo's place and allow him to use Ombwede's hut for the night with a take-away girl he had befriended at the disco.

Akuota learnt about it with disbelief when she peeped through the window in the wee hours of the following day, on hearing the couple rumbling past her window. Her investigation through Ombwede's intimate friends, like Omogo, revealed that her son had not at any one time brought a girl to his hut to break the *osuri,* hut finial.

Akuota shared the sad news with Achola, who equally regretted. They took the bull by its horn and involved the boy in a two hours counseling session attended by Akondo and Akuom to destroy seeds of disaster that would be sown if Ombwede was the second man to bring a girl to his own simba.

The solution was to immediately get an expert to give him *manyasi,* antidote, or demolish the hut and build another one for the boy.

Omogo, ever delighted by the miseries of others rubbed his hands in glee as he prepared to demolish Ombwede's hut. He jumped up and down, punching the air with excitement, patting Ombwede's back, yelling taunts and mocking him.

"*Otoyo*, hyena! Today is today! We want to demolish you today! You and your sister will sleep on the same mat in the kitchen! Apisy will write a poem about you! *Otoyo*, you slept in class! Somebody from far has taught you a lesson!" He kept following Ombwede with such irksome remarks, even as the boy who was busy grazing his mama's cow in front of their gate tried to avoid him.

In a fit of pique, Ombwede pulled down a stem of a tree and showered his back with three strong strokes of the cane. Akuota's open air benches from where the boys could clearly be seen had no customers at that particular time who could separate them.

Achola heard the commotion and decided to peep through the kitchen window with an aim of joining the fray in case Omogo overpowered her brother.

103

Ombwede twined his arms round Omogo's legs and tied them together into one unit. He hefted him shoulder high and flung him to a tree stump which inflicted grievous injuries to his waist. Ombwede came back to his senses when he learnt that his enemy, oinking on the ground like a pig had become unconscious. Ombwede vanished into the shrubs near his grazing field, leaving the cow to roam freely.

"*Choke!* What is it, Omogo?" Achola yelled, conjuring a false scowl on her face to feign anger as she moved closer to Omogo who was limping with his two hands propped on his waist.

"What's it, brother? Tell me please! Did Okebe beat you?" Achola asked, fighting back an upsurge of laughter.

"Please hold my hand and help me go back home," Omogo whimpered.

Omogo hobbled on his way back home as if he had gulped down ten glasses of *andiwo*. His injured waist forced him to walk with a stoop, like Akondo and his lover sauntering across the village in their sunset honeymoon.

"Your brother didn't allow me to prepare for war. He beat me because he caught me unaware; otherwise, that pimply boy could see fire," Omogo bragged.

"Andiwo seller! Sihoho transmitter! Husband snatcher! *Hududu fuong'*! Your cow is destroying my crooops!" Akoko's noise penetrating the air from her maize farm across the stream forced Achola to ditch Omogo and run to save the situation.

"Sorry Mama," she apologised and goaded the cow back home. Achola felt amused by Akoko's last words; *hududu fuong'*. She knew from Akuom's teachings that it was a nasty word to a woman who had lost her virginity before getting married. It was mainly applied by grannies who grew up in the days when most girls got married with their virginity intact. Achola's generation laughed off the insult considering a spoilt generation where it was almost impossible to get a girl who could maintain her virginity to the day she got married, probably...? Adoyo? But who knew, she could be having affairs elsewhere outside the vicinity of Nyakonja village? Lack of evidence left Adoyo standing solely like a grain of rice in a sack of soiled wheat.

Akuota's benches were already half occupied by customers, who were chanting praises to Ombwede for his victory an hour later in his absence.

Okong'o, seated next to a humped customer, was celebrating full psychological recovery. He had for quite long lived with the shame of being beaten in full glare of village beauties, including the ones he

105

admired. His dream of getting someone who could beat up Omogo had come true. He harboured no grudges against Okebe, whose cause for anger was clearly understood.

Omogo's stories dominated discussions as they dawdled over their drinks, hoping Okebe would pop in any time sooner. Ogoma, the village punching bag, did not go untouched, especially at that time that Okebe had not arrived.

"Where was he during the tussle?" the humped drunkard whispered with his mouth pointing Akuota's main house, where the wife inheritor was resting in the bedroom. He waited until Akuota turned her back to go back to the house for more andiwo before whispering the question out of her earshot.

"What do you expect that grouch to do?" Achola whispered back.

Akuota, who had gone to the market during the fight became word deficient over the issue, although she was worried about the whereabouts of her son who had not re-surfaced.

Okong'o cracked saucy jokes with Akuru, a woman seated next to Achola in front of the kitchen. He spoke with a re-loaded ego. His shame vanished when news broke that Ombwede had trounced Omogo.

Okong'o's jokes with the woman whose husband died a year earlier were not empty; they had strings attached. He was better placed to inherit the widow than some interested guys around the village. Her deceased husband was his cousin; a blood relationship that made him the best suitor, according to culture. Although divorced, he had his own home, just like the woman, two adolescent daughters and a ten-year-old son.

The woman gave a mild resistance to his advances. She remoulded her image into more of a lover than a drunkard. Her eyes were narrowed to slits. Her voice transformed from the crooked, croaking voice of a drunkard to the sultry voice of a smitten village beauty.

Buoyed by the spirit of victory, the two sneaked away from the hubbub to a secluded, leafy hideout behind Akuota's kitchen. Achola, who seemed to be aware of the new development, diverted her concentration to the progress. She stole glances from her seat and took the role of providing unsolicited security service.

She roared at drunken customers who were trying to weave their way to the direction of the couple's hideout for short calls, and redirected them to the shrub behind her mama's house, near Odhialo's grave.

"That place is not a urinal! The stench is too much for users of this kitchen!" she barked.

Achola lowered her stance when she spotted Okong'o leaping over an anthill, followed by the widow. They disappeared through the path leading to the widow's home.

Akuota, who grasped something from her observation, moved away from the crowd and craned her neck over the fence, probably to watch over the new couple planting seeds for another sunset honeymoon.

Akuota had good reasons for supporting their intention to fill the gaps. A man of Okong'o's age living without a wife was disastrous to the community. His eldest daughter, who took charge of the family's domestic chores after separation of her parents, was carrying a burden too heavy for her.

Okong'o's irresponsible drinking habits forced his daughter to involve in offering caretaker services reserved for a woman in the capacity of her mother, say a step-mother, an inherited widow or father's girlfriend.

He would succumb to alcohol and lie in the open, his mouth agape, bare-chest, doing all the silly stuff irresponsible drunkards do, a situation that would force the eldest child to spruce him up and carry him to his house, with the help of the other siblings.

At times, they'd be lumbered with the uneventful burden of washing him when he became grungy. Doyens of culture recommended cleansing for the bachelor's children; otherwise, they'd be inflicted with *chira*. The situation was worse in the days he was ailing from Okebe's beating.

Akuota's other reason for celebrating the relationship was the row about Ogoma's permanent stay at her home. His departure was overdue.

It was in order, according to fabricated culture, for one to leave a widow's home after performing all the rites required for the cleansing of the widow and resume his own family responsibilities.

Widows around the village were also not in good terms with Akuota for holding 'their man' for too long. Okong'o could be another hot cake on the prowl if Ogoma refused to leave Akuota's home.

The community had no issues with Akondo and Akuom's relationship. Theirs was considered to be a re-marriage but even if not, the young generation had no interest in them.

***

Akuota felt relieved on seeing her son from the kitchen in good health the following morning. He had spent the night with the girls in the kitchen to avoid the disasters from seeds he had sown on his own.

The house earmarked for demolition remained vacant with his beddings inside. He had to wait for his cultural advisors to instruct him on how to go about the whole process. He acted fast after getting assurance from his mama that everything was re-usable, apart from the building. Armed with a panga to protect him against Omogo, he ran around the village to mobilise youths, who came and demolished the hut in the twinkle of an eye.

Another man, who was more expensive than Omogo, built a new hut near the rubble of Ombwede's first hut with support from well-wishers, who gave donations with warnings against 'dosing in class' next time.

Achola's fear for the life of her mild mannered seventeen-year-old brother prompted her to act on his behalf. She found herself in hot soup when she tried to reach out to Apisy, whose granddaddy, Akondo, and aunt, Adoyo, joined hands to fend off the drunkard who was determined to subject the minor to defilement. Achola narrated to her peers that she had never known Akondo as being such a brute when it came to defending a school going girl. She apologised to Akondo, who informed her that he was annoyed in consideration to the minor's age and the blood relationship Ombwede and she shared, being members of the same clan.

"Pick one from those who sleep in that kitchen with my daughter. Some of them don't belong to our clan and they're ripe for harvesting," Akondo said with a chuckle.

Achola's brother diverted his focus to the other ladies, sparing Adoyo and Amami, who belonged to his Kaluo clan. The word tussle that ensued among the targeted girls on that night revealed their level of thirst for the underage boy.

"You'll bewitch the young man with the sins of your divorce-oriented lifestyle," Achando snarled at Apudo.

"Why can't you marry that man whose skin shines like a torch at night?" Apudo fired back at Akelo.

Achola was unperturbed by the age of her peers, who were above twenty. Her aim was to use one of them as a stepping stone, just for a night and set free the pimply underage Ombwede to look for his agemate some time in future.

Akumba, who was not sorry for the fight between the two boys, citing her brother's bad character, told Achola openly to give them husbands and stop using them as cultural pawns.

"He's no better than boys who walk for miles in the inky darkness of the night to look for girls. Tell him to wake up!" she told Achola.

CHAPTER ELEVEN

Akuota joined the frenzied group of *ohangla* dancers celebrating in commemoration of Okebe's late mother in his father's home. Organisers of the overnight *ohangla* jig paid Akuota to bring her products in large supplies. The ceremony gave her some reprieve from the rowdy drunkards yelling in her compound for whole days. It was her day off stress, to at least dance and yell out her frustrations like others.

Charged by two glasses of her own supplies, her sense of ethics code went offline. She gyrated weirdly to the beats of the drums. The shell clasped in her left armpit had some tickling effects that made her laugh cheekily, like an idiot. Akuota's weird dancing style deprived her daughter of the freedom to enjoy dancing as her peers did. Achola was too embarrassed to join the crowd of dancers where her mother was messing up, recklessly knocking people and laughing loudly like a fool.

Akuota had never been a fan of alcohol. She could only taste it to prove to her customers that it was brewed devoid of alcohol poisoning. But she was the worst of all drunkards on a day she decided to drink like any other fool.

Achola feared for her reputation on that occasion attended by some of her boyfriends. She joined Akondo and Akuom on a raised bank of earth stretching out round Onyoyo's main house, what they fondly referred to as verandah or *branda* in vernacular pronunciation, a vantage that afforded full view of the dancers. Akondo's bald surrounded by his grey hair glistened in the bright moonlight like an odourless well surrounded by burnt long grass still having fresh ash.

Akuom's stick of cigarette clasped in her tight smoke coated lips induced spoonfuls of saliva that she kept spitting onto the ground in front of their seat.

The drum player sang in praise of the most aggressive dancer of the night: "Akuota, hold his waist! Hold your man! Hold his waist!" he sang.

"Ogomaaaah…Ogoma!" the crowd jeered.

Achola sprang to her feet to inquire what the heck it was that had sent all the dancers yelling and shouting at her mama with remarks suggesting something was amiss beneath the flap of her flowery blouse around the waist.

"Is it magic or ornamental?" they kept asking as they danced around her in circles.

The vigorous gyration of Akuota's waist tossed the pig-bone up and down, exposing it to the public. Some of Achola's friends tittered amid whispers and fingers pointing at Akuota's waistline. Tickled by the shell in her armpit, the excited Akuota raised her voice above the hubbub.

At the far end of the compound adjacent to the fence was Achando, huddled together with Ombwede. She kept the boy busy with whispers to his ears, her right arm twined around his waist in a manner that drew the attention of gossipy observers milling around them to glean some information about the relationship between the girl and a boy many years her junior.

Omogo who re-surfaced for the first time since their tussle with Ombwede stood at a secluded place near a bulb powered by a generator, neither talking nor giddy with his trade-mark excitement, his right hand constantly pulling a cap to cover black scabs of recovering wounds that smudged parts of his forehead as a result of the fight.

Achola's strongest headache was her mother's acrobatics on the dance ground. Akuota gulped down more glasses of the free drink until she succumbed to the power of her own products. She wobbled towards the exit behind Onyoyo's house and collapsed near the fence.

Achola followed her mama for security against crooks and, most important, to know more about the bone dangling from her waist. She kept her in a good sleeping position and squatted to study the bone at a close

114

range. A keen look at the magic bone triggered fiery bullets of curiosity from Achola's tank of family secrets.

Something hard, like a stone, hit Achola's hand as she tried to turn her mama to one side. She untied the strap used for fastening Akuota's blouse and encountered a shell that glittered like gold trapped by the strap. It had long dropped from her armpit and clung to the strap fastened over her blouse.

She studied it closely and felt something queer in the umbilical cord tying her to her mama. She left the bone intact but withheld the shell for interrogation later when her mom would be sober.

Achola's arrogance kept nosy first aiders at bay, stopping them from accessing crucial details of her mama's magic weapons. She knew from her drinking experience that the cold night breeze blowing across her mama's chest would soon blow away the alcohol in her brain.

The dance grew livelier as the night progressed, mostly after the departure of Akuota who, according to lovers of peace, had been a public nuisance.

Achola gave a mild resistance to the weary Akondo and Akuom, who intervened to support Akuota on her way back home, considering that Akuota's home was adjacent to the path leading to Akondo's home.

They were equally frustrated by the embarrassments caused by Akuota after consuming the free alcohol, but things went beyond their control. The couple helped Akuota to walk back home without fear of meeting a night-runner because Ratila was enjoying the *ohangla* dance at Okebe's home.

Akuota woke up at dawn feeling as if somebody had planted shards of a broken glass in her joints. Her inheritor, who never attended the ceremony informed her that it was 1am local time when she returned. She had vivid memories of people shouting out the name Ogoma in his absence when her dance was at the peak the previous night.

She lifted her skirt to find out the cause of pain in her waist and saw a narrow line of fresh glowing red wound caused by the pig-bone when she had crumbled down the previous night before Achola rushed to her rescue. She gulped down a mug of water to re-hydrate her body. Akuota lost her wits after learning that the magic shell was nowhere within her body. She popped out of her house but made a step backwards on seeing Achando's skirt flapping behind her as she escaped through the fence from Ombwede's hut.

Akuota ambled on the path leading to Okebe's home with her eyes fixed on the ground, just in case the magic shell had dropped. She was certain that no serious pedestrian would pick up that shell unless they had visited a medicine man to tell them the value of such stuff. But even so, every patient could only use magic prescribed in accordance with their particular problem, not any shell for anybody as is the case with bread bought from the shop.

She dashed into the compound of the nursery school where a night-runner had scared village beauties walking on their way to her home some time back and trotted towards a group of playing kids, who fled helter-skelter at the sight of her. They screamed for help, running towards their teacher, seated in front of their classroom.

"Kindly help me if you see any of them playing with a shell, I'll reward you," the devastated Akuota pleaded with the youthful female teacher when she got to her.

"What kind of shell is it?" the teacher asked, "And what's its use?"

"Sparkling grayish, spangled with bright star-like dots. It's ornamental. I use it to adorn my table when I have visitors," she answered with an unnatural stammer depicting guilt.

"It's OK. I'll try my best," the teacher promised with a mirthless grin.

The shell believed to have some influence on the gods of the sea would punish Akuota if she failed to recover it in good time. Something kept nagging at the back of her mind concerning her fate of the day. The loss that short-circuited her memories propelled her to move on irrespective of the first person she had first met that morning. She paused by the roadside near Akuom's home to recollect the first person she had met.

The mirror of her memories brought forth Akoko, harvesting maize from her farm across the stream, singing her trademark brazen songs. But that was different from meeting someone: She had merely spotted her in her farm across the stream.

She remembered quite vividly that she had met Omogo's mother carrying a bucket of water on her head. She had recoiled from the woman who was still sulking over the fight that left her son reeling in pain for a whole week.

She ignored or rather forgot about the doctor's instructions and went ahead in her endeavour to recover the magic shell.

A medley of twists of the tongue, producing a sweet romantic whistle behind Akuom's fence, came from none other than Akondo, alerting his lover that her 'honey' was around and about. Akuota rose from her hideout to meet the old man for a word of greeting and to ask if, by chance, they had rescued the shell while supporting her to wobble back home the previous night.

"Good morning, daughter," Akondo, who was craning his neck over Akuom's fence wheeled around and greeted Akuota on hearing her footsteps.

"God bless you for your sympathy. I am sorry, it was the influence of free alcohol," Akuota appreciated.

"No problem. But are you OK?" Akondo asked. He stooped to position his right ear close to her mouth for a word she wanted to whisper.

"I lost my magic shell," Akuota whispered in tears.

Akondo turned his face to the sky, rolled his eyes like navigation compasses, stooped to the ground and wetted his wrinkled cheeks with a trickle of tears. He held Akuota's hand and whispered: "Take heart, daughter! You've lost a shield, but don't worry.''

"I wish I had known,'' he intoned, "I could have rescued it in good time. But we took you to your house and handed you over to your man. I was in hurry to escort Akuom to her home. She had requested to spend the night alone in her home. On my way back, I was alone, walking in fear of Ratila, the piti-piti man."

Akuota greeted Akuom, who had popped out of a gap in her fence and vanished to give way for the privacy of the aged couple.

The next suspect was Achola, who could not respond well to the twaddle of her mother's superstition. But she had to conjure the best approach to her daughter.

"Kindly allow me to see you privately," Akuota beckoned Achola, who was having a chat with Amami in their kitchen.

"What's it?" Achola asked arrogantly, following her mama towards a secluded place behind their fence.

"Kindly assist me,'' she said. "Did you ever see some shell drop off my body last night when I was overpowered by alcohol?" Akuota had lowered her tone to that of a beggar but Achola made good use of the opportunity to reprimand her mother.

"Are you aware you're denting the reputation of our family? Mama?" Achola asked scowling her face into a warrior.

"I am sorry, daughter; it was the influence of free alcohol," Akuota pleaded.

"Were you the only beneficiary of the free alcohol?"

"No, daughter! But have some courtesy for the woman who breastfed you," Akuota pleaded.

"Do you mean courtesy to sing praises when you behave like a spoilt village girl? That racket of drunkards shouting out your name in public? Imagine, I am too traumatised by the last night's experience."

Achola lifted her nose to the sky to sneer at her mother.

"Daughter, that's a gone case that cannot be reversed. Let's forget the past. Kindly just assist me."

"What was the use of the shell?" Achola asked.

"The shell is ornamental."

Achola suppressed an upsurge of laughter. She walked off, feigning anger in her facial expression. She said as she went, "I'll go asking the kids around but if we don't get it, I'll buy one for you, better ones are sold at Ng'iya on market days," she pouted, flailed her hands and left.

Akuota's heart pounded her ribcage with a force that could possibly unhook her soul.

Two days after the mess, Akuota could not trace her magic shell. Her style of grilling playing children in her pursuit earned her the new title of a *sihoho* transmitter, adding more evidence to Akoko's claims. Gossips had field days spreading news of a new *sihoho* transmitter on the prowl targeting children.

Akuota spotted a group of children in a play field on a misty Saturday morning pushing small round metals on the ground to enjoy driving them like cars – vruuuum! She engaged them in a race that left a burning effect between her thighs as if somebody had vigorously brushed red pepper on the surfaces of both sides.

121

"Yore. yore.. yore.. the *sihoho* transmitter in action *yore....yore....yore...yore..!"* Akoko, standing in her raised maize farm that gave her a good vantage to view the landscape shouted to mobilise the public against her.

Akuota found herself in the hands of irate community members who ganged up against her for public flogging. Ombwede threatened to die with his mother. He threw kicks and blows randomly at people who were baying for his mother's blood.

Achola, on the other hand, forced her way through the crowd to shield her mama, hurling insults and threatening to do unholy acts that would result in curses. She dared anybody who believed he was man enough to throw the first stone at her mother. She grasped the hand of a woman who was busy interrogating Akuota, yanked her by the waist and rolled with her several times on the ground sending the crowd into a scamper.

"That's the power of the pig-bone on her waist!" Pong', a mad man, unperturbed by Achola's threats stood a short distance shouting at Akuota, who was walking on her way back home flanked by her two defensive children.

"Shut up! The spirits of people you killed are haunting you!" the enraged Achola retorted.

Achola felt grieved by the challenges her mother was going through in her endeavours to recover the magic shell. Keeping it any longer would lead to the loss of the only parental figure she had after losing her dad to the cruel hands of death. She organised for an impromptu discussion with Amami, who had an inkling concerning the whole issue.

The two beauties decided to kill either a rat or a frog and deposit it under Akuota's sofa in her main house together with the magic shell from where Akuota would pick it up when she went there to get rid of the stinking carcass.

By virtue of nature, the squeamish girls would cringe away from such creatures. Ombwede would do a better job if involved. Achola crept to Ombwede's hut after making this conclusion, just before retiring to her mat but she recoiled at the voice of a girl likely to be Achando, suffocating her brother with love.

Ombwede responded positively to his sister's revelation and request the following day when she visited him in the morning in the absence of his soulmate. He tried his luck in Akondo's main house, repurposed into a cereal store due to cultural restrictions, but the old man spent a better part of the day in his *duol* having fun with Akuom. He could easily spot Ombwede entering the house and subject him to interrogation.

As a good hunter, he went on an errand that reeled three jumbo-sized rats belonging to a breed that could only be found in the darkest part of the bush dominated by deadly wild beasts. Their size almost doubled the size of ordinary rats stealing grains from Akondo's deserted house. He waded through a reedy swamp that watered Akoko's vegetable garden next to her maize farm and caught some three green frogs.

Ombwede's catch, killed and wrapped in a tattered sack, had to wait until darkness enveloped his land lest he encountered prying eyes.

Ombwede scurried through tortuous paths across the village in the darkness, carefully avoiding exposure of any kind that could attract the mob that had almost lynched his mother earlier. He jumped over Okong'o's anthill, swerved through the drunkards' urinal and made his way to the kitchen.

Enchanted by Ombwede's parcel, Amami and his sister nuzzled him dearly with words of praises. They branded him a hero and the pillar of their home.

They cringed away from the sight of dead rats and frogs, forcing Ombwede to take the plan to its next level. The sound of Ogoma snoring in the bedroom like the road man's tractor assured him of enough security. He clung to the rafters of his mother's house and aimed at the space between the wall and the sofa dropping his catch one by one until the floor beneath the sofa was littered with the rotting dead rats and frogs. He dropped the shell in the same manner and crept to his hut.

***

"Eat, my dear! Please eat! The chicken is well fried! Please eat!" Ogoma shrugged at Akuota's plea to convince him to eat the delicious chicken meal for lunch.

"I've told you I can't eat with that stench in my breathing system," he retorted and shrugged.

Akuota sniffed around the house and located the source of the stinking enemy of her love. She squatted and spotted some huge dead rats and frogs decomposing under her sofa. She turned the sofa upside down and...marvelous! A blessing in the storm! Her magic shell was gleaming atop some rotting dead rats and frogs.

But just before celebration, how did it happen? Akuota's big question remained unanswerable. On that specific night, Akondo and his lover escorted her to the house. She wondered how the shell could fly from her armpit to the floor behind her sofa. A close study of the rats failed to establish their authenticity. They were bigger and shaggier, with well trimmed stripes of glistening thick black fur running parallel to their eyelids that created a total dissimilarity to the local breeds running anyhow around the village.

125

The finicky Ogoma became shaky, looking straight into the eyes of his lover. The foul smell of the stuff was hazardous to the life of the entire family if, in any case, it had some links with witchcraft.

With the sofa laid upside down, the expensive meal on the table and the bewitched mixture of recovered shell, dead rodents and frogs on the floor, the astonished couple locked the door and rushed to Akondo's *duol*.

"Let's look for a witchdoctor," Akondo suggested.

Going back to the medicine man who gave Akuota the shell would be a mammoth task in terms of distance and logistics. The two couples rushed to Achwiya's place for help. The elderly female doctor praised Akuota for refusing to touch the bewitched stuff and advised them to pick her when everybody in the village was asleep apart from Ratila and the romantic stone throwers.

The couple whiled away the day in Akondo's *duol* discussing the dangerous encounter until 10pm local time.

Akuota's cat, which was still licking the table after devouring the generous offer, jumped to the rafters of her roof and disappeared.

"You see! Even our greedy cat could not eat the rats for all those days," Akuota whined.

"Domestic animals have an innate ability to sense witchcraft. They can't eat food that's bewitched," Achwiya explained. "Cats, particularly, have witch detectors on their whiskers."

The medicine woman sprayed some greenish liquid from a bottle she carried in her basket onto the deadly stuff. She un-wrapped a polythene paper containing some ash and sprinkled it on the same.

"Pick up your protective shell from the rot and dispose the remaining waste to your latrine pit. I'm done! One hen for the job as soon as you can find it," the doctor concluded and left.

Akuota cleaned her house and released Akondo and his Akuom, only to learn later that her son was not yet asleep. But that was a minor issue, he had no business with them since he was too engrossed in the whispers Akuota's ears could grasp from his hut. The second voice was Achando's shrill female giggles and whispers in a heightened steamy atmosphere.

Formerly a jumble of emotions, the boy's graphic line of understanding tenets of love had improved tremendously since he met Achando. His stance on Ogoma's relationship with his mother melted like wax. He had really longed to see Ogoma being hounded from his father's home the way it happened from Akoko's home when his clothes flew behind him like papers carried by a whirlwind.

Achola's effort to create a wedge between her brother and his lover hit a snag. She went around the village, complaining that Achando had refused to hand over the love she borrowed to the right suitor.

Like mother like son, Ombwede clung to the girl given to him for cultural purposes. Another breed of the sunset honeymoon where regard to HIV statuses took a back seat. Their relationship was gaining momentum and exposure like a wall poster. They developed bullet proof chests, like Ogoma's, and started doing romantic antics in full glare of the public, daring jealous observers to swallow razors and die.

CHAPTER TWELVE

The sight of the HIV/Aids crusader entering Akuota's homestead through the main gate sent cold chills down the spines of his customers. He went straight to Akuota's house for a follow-up on his first customer, Ogoma, who seemed to be doing better than the last time he was attended to. The presence of his inherited widow created conducive atmosphere for complete service delivery.

The result of the closed door voluntary counseling and testing was shocking and unbelievable according to how they understood HIV, if at all such a thing existed. Akuota, who had stayed with Ogoma for such a long time, tested negative.

They watched over her blood sample, rolling down the sample-well on the test kit with unabated breath. Akuota talked confidently, stealing glances at the blood sample inching closer to the two bars cutting across the straight line. The trail of her blood drew only one line at the end, contrary to her expectation, declaring her negative.

"Thank God but, doctor, when teaching us at the Chief's baraza you told us that the infection is sexually transmitted. How come he's positive and I'm negative?" Akuota raised her concern.

"We have cases of discordant couples, whereby one partner is negative and the other is positive depending on their sexual frequencies, resistance to infections due to cellular immunity and viral characteristics among other causes of discordance." The counselor's explanation laden with such medical jargon left Akuota floating, although with a sigh of relief.

"What should we do now that my HIV status and his are different but we continue living together as a husband and wife?" Akuota asked.

"You should remain faithful to one another and use condoms," the counselor instructed.

The couple frowned at the doctor on hearing the name of the protective sheath considered by the countryside natives as a tool for the immoral. They viewed the counselor's instructions as a violation to sex oriented cultural rights. He encouraged Ogoma to continue visiting the health centre for more HIV drugs as prescribed by health care givers.

The establishment of a new family in the home prompted Armstrong to open a new file. He moved forward to Ombwede's hut and engaged them in a closed door voluntary counseling and testing.

The counselor engaged the young couple in a professional counseling that familiarised them with the world of AIDS and living a positive and negative HIV status life. A nerve-racking silence covered Ombwede's hut as the samples of blood rolled down the test kits. The flow of Achando's blood sample across the bar on her kit ending up with two drawn lines while Ombwede's drew only one on his kit, unveiled the practicality of the existence of the virus.

They exercised the counselor's instruction to accept their statuses as they were and learn to live as such.

"It's not possible at this moment to establish your exact statuses since you've been together for less than three months. That's the window period. Kindly visit our VCT centre after three months for another test," the counselor instructed Ombwede, whose status was still hidden. He counseled Achando on living positive and linked her to Kaluo Health Centre from where HIV drugs would be administered to her.

Ombwede's love for his girlfriend was too high for such barriers to separate them. He referred to her son, Akula as 'my son' although he was aware that the boy was a product of some black deals behind walls. He felt great whenever the boy crowed with the name he loved to hear, Dad and reported petty cases of child to child conflicts to him: "So and so pinched my cheeks. Will you beat him? So and so stole my toy. Will you buy me another one?...Bla bla bla".

Achando had tangible reasons to trap such a young boy to her love basket. She was not as frigid as the demure Adoyo. Her rare figure eight shape and walking style added some value to her beauty. The light brown pigmentation on her skin glimmered in the sun like decorated leather used for covering furniture in beach hotels for tourist attraction. The wonky lines etched round her neck were natural grooves designed by her creator to make a difference between her and other female-folk claiming to personify beauty. She was almost six feet tall, the height that allowed her to view her husband like some low placed fruit she wanted to harvest whenever they walked together. Her eyebrows coiled back in a well groomed straight line pointing at a dark slit that trailed the edge of her eyelids. Fabulous! She looked more angelic than African.

Her feminine, sonorous voice inflated Ombwede's ego to get established as somebody's husband than the young boy he used to be, leave alone the government's age limit of eighteen and all those underage 'whatever'.

Achola had some wicked feelings against Achando, the girl who wanted to kill her brother with excessive love. She had coiled him into a pocket-sized object, carrying him here and there like property in her wallet, luring him with seductive self-centered demands that dehydrated her brother's body and left him withering like the leaves planted on their late father's grave but failed to take root. Achola swung around the village whining about the tick that clung to her brother's skin and could not be plucked out even when the longest nails around were applied. She complained about her naïve brother who turned wild whenever you mentioned Achando's name negatively.

But Akuota had a reason to smile. Her son's engagement was backed by culture. The girl from Kager clan was allowed to romantically mingle freely with her son from Kaluo clan. The issue of age was a none issue; her own man was five years younger, but digging hundreds of feet deep into her soul. Achola's reactions were stimulated by the alcohol in her brain, according to her mother. Her failure to clinch a husband was sending bad signals to the entire community. Sadly, she would be buried in the bush behind the home if she died, according to cultural experts, to gag spirits of singleness. An adult man who died a bachelor was to be buried with the soles of his feet pricked with thorns to gag spirits of bachelorhood, *msumba*.

***

"Why do you always feel shy when coming to your man, daughter?" Akuota asked Achando with a mischievous wink.

"Oh...no! I just...! I mean ooh...no! I'm just...! But I'm Ok...! Mama...!" The brown, figure eight, willowy girl coyly plucked leaves from Akuota's fence with her head bent at an angle expressive of true willingness to spread her roots farther and deeper into this home in a word deficiency situation.

"Kindly take a bucket and bring me some water from the spring-well," Akuota requested.

Achando responded with alacrity to Akuota's request. Akuota's encouragement whetted Achando's appetite for some more Ombwede, age-gap stashed to her armpits. She went ahead and took full responsibility as Ombwede's legitimate wife despite the mound of flesh growing bigger on Achola's cheeks due to excessive sulking. Achola desperately spoke in parables targeting her sister-in-law at the peak of village gossip to incite Akuota's customers against her, but the drunkards adhered to Akuota's gag rule supported by Okebe.

Ombwede drastically developed into a gorilla. He took the helm of defending his family, as is expected of a man.

The drinking ragtag seated on the benches in the open welcomed Ombwede to the group of adults. Having a wife elevated him to adult status. Adults allowed him to join them wherever they were and contribute to discussions on matters, adult. He had an upper hand than the twenty-year-old Omogo, who had never been heard talking about marriage even though he was an active stone thrower who disturbed maidens at their sleeping places around the village. Kids resembling Omogo could be seen playing around the teeming village although he claimed to be a father of zero.

Ombwede looked scared like a strangled goose in the midst of adults sipping *andiwo* from their glasses in his first attempt. He had never tasted alcohol before, but the latest achievements empowered him to enjoy the fruits of adulthood.

Real men went back to their houses wobbling and crooning smoochy and traditional songs of the latest hits. They enjoyed hearing their wives complaining to colleagues about how they went back home the previous night drunk and disorderly, most importantly when endeared with the name of their first-born children: the father of so and so, in Ombwede's case, the father of Akula or baba Akula.

Akuota ignored her son's coins placed on the table and served him a glass half full of free *andiwo*.

Gales of laughter erupted as Ombwede rolled from his seat as if doing a somersault and landed on the ground with his head carrying the whole body. A rescue team carried him to a shade where they applied their skills to de-alcoholise the new recruit. They fed him on raw eggs from Akuota's hatchery to induce vomit.

Achando, who had just returned from the spring-well, went berserk. She scurried to the scene and wailed loudly with angry remarks against whoever was responsible for the act. She however softened her tone on realising that her mother-in-law had contributed. She supported her man to his bed, where he succumbed to a deep slumber.

Achando developed some fear in Ombwede's decision to start drinking as a way of proving his maturity. She rushed to Akondo's *duol* for some wise counsel but found him missing. She met Omogo's mother on her way out, who informed her that Akondo was on his way to Akuom's home.

The groovy old man, who was flipping through the pages of a dog-eared magazine, welcomed her with a smile, referring to her with the title she loved most; 'my granddaughter-in-law'.

Achando expressed her fear concerning the prospects of Ombwede shirking his responsibilities if he sank deeper into alcohol. She gave examples of people like Okong'o, whose families failed because of alcohol influence. She stemmed her concern to Omogo, who almost raped his elder sister, Akumba one night under the influence of alcohol, only to be rescued by neighbours, who found her in tatters.

"Let's relish this sirloin steak. We'll give you advice jointly after killing hunger," Akondo requested the young woman as Akuom arranged the plates on the table.

Achando took over from Akuom by quickly serving the old couple. They chatted happily, belching with satisfaction and relief. Akuom, who had got wind of Achando's woes, changed the venue of the counseling to her late husband's *duol*, which was still in good condition, to enhance privacy.

"Well, listen to me, granddaughter. I was a drunkard for more than thirty years and I am well conversant with the vicissitudes of living with a drunkard. But I'd like you to follow the footsteps of my late wife; she never allowed my drinking habits to ruin our family. She remained tolerant and submissive. The woman screamed for help one day when my son, the late Odima, was still an infant. I had wobbled into the house and sat on the child, who was asleep in the bed, almost killing him. She yanked me by the waist and flung me to a cooking pot which broke to smithereens," Akondo narrated with a smile.

"Choke!" Achando exclaimed.

"Imagine! Therefore, you need to take heart as a wife to save your family. Some of us men are like children at times and need to be handled with lots of maturity and wisdom. Ombwede cannot be compared to village louts like Okong'o. The carpentry skills he learnt from his late father will help to sustain your family," Akondo encouraged.

"I'd pinch your cheeks if I was your wife," Akuom said with a chuckle.

Akondo's advice to his 'granddaughter-in-law' put Ombwede on the safer side. He'd live to enjoy all the benefits of having a long suffering, mature and tolerant wife, ready to embrace vagaries of living with a drunkard.

CHAPTER THIRTEEN

Ombwede trudged on his way back home, crooning self-composed smoochy songs to restore romantic equilibrium in his marriage:

> *Call it AIDS or chira…! Achando is my choice!*
> *Jealous people, swallow razors and die!*
> *Call it age or height…! Achando is my choice!*
> *Jealous people, swallow razors and die!*
> *Unmarried girls…! Look for husbands and marry!*
> *Jealous people, swallow razors and die!*

Ombwede's voice was loudly trumpeting his stand against Achola, who had an uneasy truce with her sister-in-law after failing to oust her. The message clearly reaching the ears of village gossips in the midnight breeze unleashed the stoking fire in his sister's stomach.

Achola sprang from her mat and lunged towards Okong'o's anthill to discipline her brother, who was stepping on her toes at a time she had decided to throw her wishes to the wind. She clasped her arms round his waist and flung him onto the anthill, accompanying this with kicks and blows. She held him on the ground in a firm grip and straddled him.

Amami, who followed her joined the fray. She pinched Ombwede's cheeks, giving warnings and queries pertaining to his problem with *wagogni,* daughters of the land or *mgogo* if one.

"Ombwede! I ask you Ombwede! Did you want to marry me?" the enraged Achola asked her brother, who was groaning helplessly on the anthill in the grip of two half naked girls.

"Marry me now! Ombwede marry me now! I'm telling you to marry me now! My brother, marry me now!" Achola went an extra mile by doing grievous anti-cultural gymnastics like a wizard at the peak of her witchcraft.

Scared by the ambiguous activities Achola was performing on her brother in the middle of the night, Amami ran to Akuota's house and banged her bedroom window with a shout that roused everybody in the home and neighbourhood, "Mama! Wake up, Achola is bewitching Ombwede!"

The scene of witchcraft was soon crowded by bewildered spectators, who refused to intervene but observe the new breed of youthful witch in action. Achando ran around the scene moaning appealingly for intervention to save her husband, who lay on the anthill facing the sky

140

with his mouth agape and eyes rolling as if Achola's venom had infused his blood and entire breathing system.

The half nude Achola jumped over her catch; dancing, slapping her laps, spitting on his face and cursing with toxic remarks that originated from the most notorious ancient wizards.

In a bid to save her only son from the claws of satanic forces, Akuota closed in but jerked backwards at the toxic curses never expected from a girl of Achola's age. Like a coward dog, threatening to bite, she barked at Achola: "Stop it!" but jerked backward at the sight of a possessed girl turning to her side to unleash ballistic missiles to her mother.

Amami re-surfaced in full dress, fearing for her life if she continued spending nights on the same mat with this girl who seemed to have acquired some questionable powers.

Achola came back to her senses and lifted her head. She winced at the spectators and weaved her way back to the kitchen without saying a word.

Achando joined hands with her teary mother-in-law to carry her man to his hut. The baffled crowd dispersed in grief, mouths pursed. A cool breeze swept across the village to blow away shock waves that remained still in the spines of observers, shuffling back home in sombre silence.

141

Amami braved her way all the way to Akondo's home and requested Adoyo to allow her back into their kitchen. Reason?

"You'll hear it from the villagers who rushed to the scene! I'm too embarrassed to narrate," she whined.

"I don't know! God! Odhialo was never a wizard! I wonder which devil has sown this seed of witchcraft in my daughter's blood," whined Akuota, who remained seated on her bed after the shocking incident.

"I'd have separated them if it was a normal fight! But what transpired was far beyond Achola beating Ombwede!" Akuota, wearing a long donkey face snarled.

"The words I've heard from my daughter's mouth this night are too evil for a girl of her age! But God knows! *Nyasaye wuora! Obong'o Were!*" Akuota moaned, tears rolling down her cheeks as she narrated the ordeal.

Ombwede woke up late the following day feeling as if he had been engaged in some bullfight the previous night. 9am local time, he shuffled to the fenced place of bath behind his hut to enjoy bathing in the warm water prepared by his wife.

His memory of the previous night's events was misty. He risked losing clients if he failed to do their work in time. The assignments he had for the day were manageable if he worked fast.

According to his diary, Akoko had invited him to repair her kitchen door, Omogo's mother had a broken window to be fixed and Okebe had ordered for a four-by-six inches bed.

Ombwede gulped down the mug of porridge served by his wife and rushed to Akoko's home. He fixed a dislocated hinge in less than thirty minutes and appreciated Akoko for the one hundred Kenya shillings she paid him for the job.

His entry into Omogo's home was a bit challenging since they had never reconciled but were only living on uneasy truce. He braved his way in but Omogo's effort to restrain his fierce dog from attacking Ombwede proved to him that the man harboured no grudges against him.

"Welcome, brother," Omogo greeted him and gave him a warm welcome.

Clad in short trousers, Omogo sat near him for a chat as he repaired the window.

"Do you know why I don't do maintenance for Mama?" Omogo asked.

"No, I don't know," Ombwede responded.

"She can't offer me even one *ondago* if I work for her," Omogo said with a chuckle.

"Lower your tone please, she's washing plates behind the house," Ombwede shushed, looking straight at Omogo's eyes.

"You reason as I do. Akuota will never give me even a coin if I offer to repair anything in our home. So, let's do this: if she has a similar problem, I'll feign lack of skills to allow you to do the work, and then you and I will drink together. You also do the same," Ombwede resolved.

"Of course, yes, we swap them like that," Omogo replied with a nod of assent.

Omogo's mother, known by her village name Asem, paid Ombwede eighty Kenya shillings after approving his work and left for the spring-well with a bucket dangling from her arm.

"Please come over," Ombwede beckoned Omogo.

"But don't insult people after drinking," Akumba shouted at the two reconciled friends, who vanished into the path leading to Akoko's home.

"Did you know? Akoko is back to her *andiwo* business," Ombwede informed Omogo.

"Serious!" Omogo roared in surprise.

"Yes, let's just go. You'll see for yourself," Ombwede assured him.

They swaggered to Akoko's home and settled on a bench she had re-arranged under a mango tree for her customers. Just like Akuota's place, Akoko's shade had very few customers during the morning hours, just a few village louts whose daily business was to beg for alcohol from one den to another.

"You're back, son?" Akoko asked Ombwede, sidling towards them for their orders.

"Yes. Please give us two *ondagos* each," Ombwede ordered.

"Thanks in advance," Omogo appreciated.

"Imagine, last night, I drank myself silly and left this place at around midnight. I have a hazy recollection of a feud between me and Achola. I can remember she was dancing over my drunken body like a wizard on the anthill behind our kitchen with a crowd of spectators helplessly gawping at us," he narrated.

Omogo listened, wrinkling his nose to demonstrate grief.

"What about Achando, Mama and Amami," Omogo asked.

"I can remember Amami also beating me when the quarrel started but she disappeared later," Ombwede answered.

"Let me just advise you before this place is crowded please," Akoko, who had served them alcohol, joined them on the bench and said.

"Please do," Ombwede urged.

"I watched the incident from far because you left here quietly in a group of other friends but started shouting as soon as you were out of my gate," Akoko explained.

145

"Your sister seems to have joined a group of women with some bad influence. They teach her all sorts of bad things one can do to bewitch an enemy. Women who drink have the worst influence you can imagine in this world. Your mother, to this moment, is still traumatised by the unholy acts she saw. Akuota has never been a wizard. Even the insults I hurl at her when we quarrel over the man she snatched away from me simply are anger driven. I know her as an innocent woman who knows nothing when it comes to witchcraft. I'd therefore advise you to take time and visit Akondo privately for some counseling," Akoko advised.

"But what do you think is wrong with my sister?" Ombwede asked.

"Your sister is against your marriage to Achando. She expected her to be used for breaking the *osuri* after which you had to look for a younger girl of your age to marry," Akoko explained.

"But Achando is-is-is...I tell you!" Ombwede shook his head with a mischievous wink that caused laughter to his audience.

"Just keep it with you, son, don't tell us!" Akoko whacked Ombwede on the back and walked towards her house, laughing loudly.

Akoko's return to the alcohol business was a boon to Ombwede, who didn't like drinking near his mother. At least he wanted somewhere he could yell freely. Her business had been stopped by the Chief when she threw tantrums at elders sent to settle disputes between her and Akuota a few days after she had hounded out Ogoma in the most inhuman manner.

"Tell the Chief I am not his wife!" she had shouted at the elders.

***

Achola found herself in an unfamiliar situation when everybody in the village frowned upon her after being branded a witch. Her peers, that bevy of beauties who spent their nights together in the kitchen at Akondo's home, cringed away from her company and avoided her at all costs. Children screamed on their toes wherever she went, as if they had seen a monster.

Nobody, including her boyfriends, mingled freely with her as they used to. Her own mother looked at her with some hooded eyes. Rumour mongers successfully tailored the midnight incident to link it to those days when Akuota was miserably running behind children to recover her lost magic shell. They had said she was casting spells on village kids. The pig-bone saga added more salt to the wound.

"Even if I am a witch, it's from your blood. Have you forgotten the day I saved you from the lynch mob?" Achola snarled at her mother when Akuota approached her for a detailed explanation on the incident.

She rued the night she had lost her temper and used the alcohol in her brain to do prohibited acts on her brother in public. She feared spending nights alone in her mother's kitchen. Such isolated places provided conducive atmosphere for night-runners like Ratila.

She had indeed fallen victim to Ratila's *piti-piti* night sports a number of times. At times, the night-runner would enter the kitchen in form of a cloud of darkness that would cover her on the mat and suck her strength and senses before going into his lunatic antics. A harsh cloud of cold dust would sweep across her half dead body followed by grotesque images in human form spitting on her face and whispering taunts laden with silly grins to demonstrate the pleasure they had in performing their duty: *"Girl! Tonight, we'll work on you – Ahaha-hihihi-uuwih-hai-hayah."* And dancing around her body joyfully singing in Swahili language distorted by mother tongue supremacy: *"Leo ni leo, leo sisi anakuta wewe, leo ni leo sisi ataroga wewe (Today is today, today we've caught you, today is today we'll bewitch you)."*

Ratila was believed to be an army of ghosts incarnated in human form. Rumours from people walking at night for various reasons like young couples penetrating darkness for illicit intentions but fell in his trap midway had it that the man would balloon himself to a dark huge bushy figure, cover them and evaporate their strengths and senses before performing on them. He'd do lunatic acts like peeing on their faces and tickling them before releasing them with a farewell message: "Safe

148

journey dear ones." Acts that left them scampering to safety in different directions only to trace each other the following day to ask the state of affairs.

Achola tried several times to appease his spirits by offering free *andiwo* as a bribe for leniency but the situation just worsened.

She thought of leaving the village to a far-off place, such as her aunt's home in Yimbo, where Amami had stayed for some time. But the sad news had reached Akondo's sister.

Akuota avoided rubbing shoulders with her daughter, a custodian of some crucial information.

***

Dangerous seeds of disaster sowed by Ombwede's sister prompted him to visit Akondo in his private room.

"Just take heart, young boy. In case you acquire *chira* resulting from the heinous acts, contact me. We'll see what to do. It's too early as for now to prescribe an antidote for you before seeing signs," Akondo instructed.

"But I've seen some signs that I can't understand. My wife vomits all the time. She's too picky in the types of food she eats. She looks very tired and bored," Ombwede explained.

"Ahahahaa! My boy, that's a blessing from God! We hope to see a new member of this community in less than a year's time. Kudos to you!" Ombwede was jazzed by the revelation.

"And let me teach you something. When you'll have your home in future, you'll build Akula's house on the left-hand side of your main house facing the gate, OK?" Akondo instructed.

"But the first-born's house is supposed to be on the right-hand side!" Ombwede complained.

"Listen to me, young man. If you build his house on the right-hand side of your main house, he'll deprive your biological children of their blessings. Remember, the boy is illegitimate," Akondo warned.

Ombwede left Akondo's home through the gap in the fence behind his main house and strode towards the main road leading to Okebe's home. He spotted a boy on the main road a short distance away in school uniform, carrying a rucksack on his way home. The face looked familiar but Ombwede refrained from shouting out his name. Okong'o's experience with Okebe was a good lesson for people who were fond of calling people by their primary school nick names.

"Vasco Da Gama! Vasco Da Dama! Vasco Da Gamaaah..!" some kids playing by the roadside ridiculed the boy using the name Ombwede didn't want to use.

150

"I'll cane you! Mannerless children!" he warned them, pointing a finger at them.

Ombwede smirked at the way the children ridiculed his former classmate with the name they gave him in Class Six because of his head, which resembled that of the historical Vasco Da Gama, whose name dominated history books.

He walked slowly some distance behind the boy to avoid the frustration of talking to someone who had left him behind in academic achievement.

Ombwede believed his failure was caused by circumstances beyond control and not his personal weaknesses. He had left school in Class Six, in third term, when his father succumbed to throat cancer. He resorted to invest in his father's carpentry career, having acquired some skills earlier.

CHAPTER FOURTEEN

Okebe's departure from his father's home to establish his own home in a field adjacent to the path leading to his father's home was another ceremonial activity that reeled a good number of community members to see him out.

The cock tethered to a tree in the field to test the security of Okebe's new settlement venue overnight was found in good condition according to culture. It would have been dangerous to settle there if a wild animal had killed the cock. In that case, the field would have been declared insecure for settlement, forcing Okebe to try his luck elsewhere.

There was traditional songs galore in the joint communal work. Omogo, the village engineer, stretched a rope on the site reserved for the first hut to be completed the same day according to the custom. He planted pegs on the spots to be occupied by the wall poles.

A trail of women bantering on their way to and fro the spring-well with buckets of water on their heads filled tanks to facilitate the activity. Energetic men soiled their bodies, digging the ground to prepare soil for baking and covering the wall. Plumes of smoke rising from three-stone fire places sent good signals to village louts who made good use of such ceremonies to fill their stomachs. Ombwede led the team that pulled out the pegs and dug holes for wall poles.

Okong'o's shoulders were sagging from the weight of bunches of reeds he carried from the stream cut by Ratila. Akelo's luminous boyfriend from Alara supplied troughs of water to the heap of soil dug by his colleagues who were baking it into clay with their feet.

A contingent of grey haired community elders arched round a table in their VIP shade had nothing to do with labour but counseling and advice. They sat comfortably, clad in their ceremonial regalia and plumed caps. They made an audit of every activity and advised Okebe accordingly wherever he went wrong. Okebe's father joined the same group to discuss sensitive issues that'd enhance Okebe's security in his new home.

Akondo, the funkiest elder in the group, kept picking blades of grass and chewing on them as if applying an antidote to some *chira* somewhere.

The track record of Okebe's activities so far was in order according to his dad's report to the elders. He had woken up at dawn the same day and gone to the site with his thirteen-year-old first-born son, Otwiyo, carrying an axe. He cut the first tree to be used as the corner pole for his hut. He dug the first hole for the pole in accordance with cultural rules and flagged off the work.

153

Okebe rushed to the site of his hut under construction to save the workers who looked stranded. Neither working nor talking. The shingled skeleton of the hut was complete and ready for the flesh that would be the wet earth and the roofing grass.

"What's it?" Okebe asked.

"Our culture dictates that the first lump of clay for covering the wall has to be placed by you followed by your wife before we continue," Akumba snarled.

Okebe scooped a lump of clay from the mass and planted it at a corner of the wall between the shingles of reeds tied round the wall poles. His wife also did the same and the rest jointly scooped lumps of clay and filled the remaining spaces as Omogo, with the help of Ombwede, thatched the roof.

Walking behind Achieno, Okebe's wife, like her shadow, was Akuom, giving her step-by-step instructions on how to go about the entire business without sowing any seed of disaster. Akuom was the one who had warned the couple against establishing their home behind their father's home as they wished. She advised Okebe that floods flowing from his home to his father's home during the rainy season could cause grievous *chira* that could kill all the members of his family, but that it was a blessing if the floods flowed from his dad's home to his home. Culture also prohibits establishing a new home when the wife is pregnant.

Cultural advisors used examples to point out the seriousness of the cultural laws. They pointed out victims of *chira* to warn their cohorts against acts prohibited by culture. *Kwero*, taboo, and *chira* dominated the discussion on the elders' table.

"What happened to Pong'? He'd be a very good boy if he were not mad," Osweta, Okong'o's father, asked the elders seated round the table with calabashes of steaming porridge on the table in front of them.

"Pong' got married to a very submissive wife from Uyoma but, seeds of disaster, his wife used his mother's broom to sweep the floor of his hut," Onyoyo answered.

The group of elders shook their heads in bewilderment at the unholy act done by Pong's estranged wife. They cursed the estranged woman and blamed her for the cultural woes bedeviling their son.

"That's the problem with our girls today. They feel they're too civilised to obey culture. Tell a girl that that's a taboo and she'll tell you that your ideas are shop-soiled," Akondo whined. "But that was a minor issue. I wish it had been brought to our table in good time. An antidote for that is available."

155

"The girl did more lunacy than just that," Onyoyo said. "There's a rainy season that she sowed seeds in her farm ahead of her mother-in-law."

"All those could have been cured if Pong' had reported them in good time, but he ignored the elders' advice and now lives to see with his own eyes. Those are seeds of disaster," Akondo concluded.

"How can we help this boy who got married recently?" Onyoyo asked.

"Ooh…well…at his age, his knowledge of our custom is still thin. Just teach him all about marriage and custom. He's more vulnerable to *chira* because of his day-to-day interactions with his in-laws," Akondo answered.

"That's the disadvantage of marrying a girl from the same village although they belong to different clans allowed to inter-marry. They share the same market, spring-well and ceremonial events like this," Onyoyo commented.

"Just look! Akondo, look!" Osweta said, pointing at Ombwede, who was busy fastening grass and throwing to Omogo on the roof.

"There he is, busy working, clad in shorts that expose his thighs to the mother-in-law."

"Where is his mother-in-law?" Akondo asked.

"There she is, at the fire place, boiling meat," Osweta said with a smile.

"*Choke!* You mean Achando's mother has been here all along?" Akondo snarled.

"Imagine!" Osweta exclaimed.

"He needs some counseling! Sincerely," Akondo concluded.

"But the girl is a good one," Onyoyo expressed.

"Very obedient and beautiful. Look at the silver bracelets round her wrist! Her sparkling brown skin! The natural rings etched round her neck! The glint in the pupils of her black angelic eyes! Her figure eight shape that wobbles freely like a camel when she walks! Marvelous!"

The groovy Akondo spoke looking admiringly at Achando, who was busy cooking together with her mother, Amoko, at the fire place. His remarks elicited gales of laughter from the elders.

"Akondo, it is unfortunate that you've grown old. If you were still in your prime, such birds could easily fall into your trap," Onyoyo said.

"I tell you, my brother!" Akondo said, shaking his head wistfully.

"But tell me, from my observation, her womb has blossomed?" Osweta inquired.

"Don't even ask, my brother. Just relax, very soon, we'll have a new member of this community," Akondo said with a chuckle.

157

"Those old men with distended bellies…! Stand up and work with other people!" Pong', who had been feasting at the same place, shouted at the village elders as he disappeared through shrubs some safe distance away from the venue.

"Hear him! Harvesting fruits of seeds he sowed," Onyoyo commented amid laughter from the elders amused by the description 'distended bellies'.

Achola, still determined to polish up her reputation, worked cheerfully with her community members. She joined the women in carrying water from the spring-well, jabbering freely with them but giving a deaf ear to anybody willing to discuss the indecent act.

Akuota, preparing chicken meal at a fire place, maintained soberness to avoid another ugly incident that'd cost her the reputation she had struggled a lot to re-build. Three jerrycans of her products were lying somewhere in a shroud of leaves, waiting for consumption as soon as the work was over. Releasing them earlier would cause messes. She wore a long, full dress to cover the magic pig-bone which exposed a mound with a sharp pointed end that protruded from under the dress whenever she bent, hence raising eyebrows from bewildered spectators. She lied to people that she had been involved in a road accident, which dislocated her hip bone.

A special dish was prepared for the village elders believed to carry the blessings that would determine the fate of the newly established home. *'When they eat and spit in your home, their saliva shower your home with bountiful blessings and prosperity'* Onyoyo's advice to his son ventilated the elders' lungs with the best air in the new compound, giving them a reprieve from hard labour and an opportunity to enjoy the best dish of all the meals prepared by their host.

Their table was flourishing with bowls of steaming chicken meat prepared by experienced women such as Akuota and Asem. The women had the profundity of knowledge of the parts of the chicken to be served to whom, depending on blood relationship to the host and title. Entrails and other dreck could elicit fierce reactions if found in the bowls placed on the elders' table.

The elders didn't spare the controversy surrounding AIDS and *chira* in their discussion. They discussed it at length to avoid misleading their disciples.

The phenomenon of queer health complications and increase in death rates across the village required some divine intervention. It was a situation that shook cultural wonks like Akondo, who bragged around with their experience in culture and *chira* prevention solutions. Akondo himself had lost many children plus his wife in compromising circumstances.

The oldies balanced between the practicality of AIDS and *chira*. The appalling mortality rate from complicated health conditions called for more than just believing in *chira*. But having no business in discussing HIV/Aids, their stories swirled around victims of *chira* who flouted culture in a way or another.

Akondo freely revealed his cultural weakness which killed grown-up children from his family, including Apisy's father.

"My wife died six months after the death of Akuom's husband, but I messed myself up by inheriting Akuom before performing all the rituals, as required by the custom," Akondo revealed.

"How?" Osweta asked.

"After burying your wife, you don't sleep in your house. You sleep outside in front of your house until you have some sweet dream about your deceased wife. I mean something romantic!" Akondo said with a chuckle.

"But what happened?" Onyoyo asked.

"I slept in the cold for a whole month but found it colourless, my dreams revolved around hunting and killing antelopes and jackals. I gave up because I was tired of sleeping in the cold, worsened by drizzles during that rainy season," Akondo explained.

"But why did you rush into another relationship before seeing an expert to help you gag those spirits of your deceased wife?" Onyoyo asked.

"Life without a woman beside you is too boring, brother. I just don't understand how you've made it for that long after the death of Okebe's mother," Akondo wondered.

"It's possible as long as you act your age, Akondo," Onyoyo assured.

"I know what an enemy in the funeral committee did to the body of your wife to divert your dreams to hunting," Osweta offered.

"Tell me please," Akondo requested.

"They wrapped the body with an *ang'uola*, underwear, before dressing her in her burial gown," Osweta jazzed his colleagues with the revelation.

"But that's just a piece of cloth like a pant! How does it block those sweet dreams about your wife?" Onyoyo asked.

"The angel of death recognises bodies wrapped with *ang'uola* as fully dressed people in the spirit world and restrain them from visiting spouses in their dreamland," Osweta elucidated.

Osweta's revelation concurred with that from the witchdoctor who had treated Akondo after losing his fourth child, a daughter. The same doctor who gave Akuota the pig-bone and other magic stuff plus tough conditions that kept her behaving like a crazy woman or a wizard.

But Akondo never wanted to unveil his experience with the witchdoctor, visiting witchdoctors is a confidential issue. He revved up his memory of those who had handled the body of his wife many years earlier to know who had sown the seed of disaster that killed his children plus one daughter-in-law, Apisy's mother. Two sons buried with thorns pricked to the soles of their feet, because they were bachelors at the time of their demise, and one daughter buried behind the home according to the custom because she was a *mgogo*.

Men were declared innocent. They're not allowed by culture to dress up dead women. In his vivid memory, Odhialo's late mother, who had died in her early eighties, one year after burying his (Akondo's) wife, had led the team of women who dressed up the body. His sister, married in Yimbo, had also been in the group. Onyoyo's late wife also featured although he never wanted to inform the old man, for the sake of peace. Achwiya, who later became his traditional doctor, amongst others, had also been there. Akondo, in his wisdom, used parables to attack the suspects.

"If you blow out a speck from somebody's eye today, the same eye will bewitch you tomorrow," Akondo whined.

"Which eyes are you referring to?" Onyoyo asked with admonitory glances, his vivid memory revealing clearly that his late wife was a participant in the controversial funeral activity.

"Not-not a quarrel my brother because the dead cannot be brought back to life," Akondo pleaded on seeing a red hue running zigzag across Onyoyo's eye.

"Akondo! Did you come to my son's new home to sow some seeds of disaster?" Onyoyo growled.

"But who mentioned your name? Do men dress bodies of dead women?" Akondo roared back, bracing to prove his mettle as a man. Too much pleading would make him a coward, worse, in the presence of Akuom, who was still busy guiding Okebe's wife.

Osweta rose to the duty of controlling the fiery exchange between the two old men, which would possibly cause fist-fight.

"Osweta, get it from me! When Odima's mother died, my late wife was in the group of women who dressed the body. I therefore feel touched when this fellow talks of some eyes that are bewitching him. Listen! Akondo is my cousin! I… Onyoyo…to bewitch my own blood…?" Onyoyo relapsed to a moaning victim of character assassination.

163

"Old man, stop quarrelling my guests!" Okebe, who realised that something was amiss, lunged towards his dad in the elders' shade and ordered.

"OK, let me leave if you don't want me in your home, son!" Onyoyo stomped the ground with his walking stick and got up to leave but Akondo turned on him with a plea for the safety of Okebe, considering the curses he'd leave behind if he left the new home in a huff, worst of all if he spat on the soil of his son's home in a cursing manner. A spoonful of the cursed saliva would cost lives in the home.

"Don't do that, brother! Please don't go! That was a minor issue, Onyoyo! Please just sit!" Akondo and Osweta jointly requested Okebe's father.

"But why is he chasing me away from his home like a dog? A seed from my waist…?" Onyoyo clicked his tongue and succumbed to the plea of his peers.

"Let's do this please," Osweta requested. "My wife is ailing even as we sit here. I think we're through with the business of this home. I'd like the two of you to go with me for a word of prayer for Okong'o's mother."

"He should learn to rehabilitate his peers! Not quarrelling all the time with our community elders," the no-nonsense Okebe muttered to himself authoritatively as the elders shuffled together on their way out to Osweta's home.

The elders' departure from the new home was long overdue. They were only required to bless the home at the initial stages of the launching and eat the parts of the hen reserved for them, spit some spoonfuls of blessed saliva and leave for the labourers to continue with their work.

CHAPTER FIFTEEN

Tired of begging for love from unwilling local widow inheritors, Akoko joined the troop of traders on her way to Ng'iya market on a market day in the guise of buying some goodies for domestic use. The ear breaking clamour of humanity and cattle for sale enlivened the business hub. She wandered here and there in every corner of the market, haggling over prices of goods she never intended to buy.

 Running queer errands in a market packed with thousands of buyers and sellers was the most challenging experience Akoko was going through in her endeavour to clinch a soulmate.

The long-distance walk from her village to the open-air market would not go with negative results; she had to, at least, acquire some guy to extricate herself from constant tussle with Akuota over Ogoma.

It was not in order for a woman to approach a man with a proposal for a romantic relationship. For social decorum to take its course, men were expected to take that kind of initiative. But Akoko played her cards with several men in the village cleared by cultural technocrats to take up the ball from Ogoma. She found them colourless. They gave her side glances and stepped out of her way whenever she stretched out her toes to play her romantic foot-sie.

Akoko rued the day she chucked out Ogoma from her compound, hurling at him all sorts of insults one can imagine. The inhuman act instilled fear in the hearts of lovers who would otherwise have replaced Ogoma in a smooth transition.

The tranquil wife inheritor had won sympathy from village stake holders who used their influence to warn all lovers against Akoko.

Akoko's decision to walk for a long distance for a blind date would be frowned upon by cultural experts from her husband's clan, but she didn't care. It was a last resort after waiting for too long.

Stories from regular visitors of the market about the tin-kickers of Ng'iya prompted Akoko to try her luck. Drovers and other business people dealing in farm products told Akoko of how single women got their lovers from the deal that required no seduction but just moving towards a range of tins and kicking one of them. The owner of the tin, by virtue of right, would pop out of his hideout and claim the woman that had kicked the tin.

Empowered by a law enacted by the locals to match widows and widowers, widowers carried empty tins to the market centre and lined them up. They hovered in the background watching their tins.

A widow like Akoko was advised to kick one of the tins, unaware of who owned it. Culture recognised the owner of the tin as the legitimate inheritor of the woman who kicked the tin, irrespective of whether the woman loved him or not.

Akoko's eyes scanned around to ensure that none of her villagemates was around. Unaware that Osweta, who was in the same market to buy some herbal medicine for his bedridden wife was watching her, she sidled towards the range of tins and kicked one of them like a footballer.

A weary old man, who had been reclining on a tree trunk, rose from his jolly and shuffled towards Akoko. He was as old as Akoko's father-in-law, days before his demise. His face resembled that of *Homohabilis*, about which Akoko learnt in her history classes on evolution of man. His jagged, jigger infested fingers and toes resembled her late husband's wrecked rake disposed at the junk yard behind her fence. His scattered golden-brown teeth seemed to have an allergy for the toothbrush. A thick oily layer on the surface of his skin gave a clear audit of the day he had had a quarrel with water and swore, with his belly on the ground, that they'd never meet. The tatters covering his body in the name of clothes seemed to have been soaked in cowdung before the old man left his home in pursuit of a soulmate.

Akoko recoiled from his gorilla smile and declined his crooked hand stretched out for a word of greeting. Fear of the wrath of cultural law enforcers prompted Akoko to follow the man to his home. But she did her usual lunatics by giving Akuota's details during introduction: "My name is Akuota. My address is the late Odhialo. I come from Nyakonja village,'' she said deliberately to cause trouble to her rival whenever Akuota would go to the same market. She knew that the old man's ancient-looking feet were too weak to carry him to Nyakonja village but he would keep asking people from the village on market days to help him trace the woman.

She dumped the hen offered by the old man for a welcome feast and crossed the fence, weaved her way out of the village and trekked back home.

***

Akoko borrowed a leaf out of Achando's book, the lady who successfully sank her roots deep into the heart of a boy many years her junior. She drew her claws to one of her clients who seemed to fear the burden of keeping a legitimate wife, a common weakness of most wife inheritors.

She offered Omogo a whole glass of *andiwo* as the first step in her endeavour to start making inroads into his heart. She invited him more frequently for repairs and meals. She cracked saucy jokes with Omogo and spruced up her hoarse alcoholic voice into a sultry voice.

Special dishes prepared for Omogo at odd hours anchored him more easily on Akoko's pillar than day time entertainment, considering the young man's shyness in the presence of a crowd.

Fried chicken dish at 10pm on the table to his honour turned Omogo into an idiot. Akoko shielded him from the wrath of jealous drunkards by informing her clients that no alcohol would be sold after 9pm, because the Chief had sent her a warning note. Some agile customers sensed the latest development and whispered it to their cronies.

Omogo was seized by the fangs of the dragon the night he gulped down one glass of *andiwo* after the meals, and succumbed to the fondling touch of the spongy hands of the woman. He woke up in the wee hours of the following day only to realise that he had taken full responsibility as the owner of the home.

But call him inheritor, call him all the stuff they use to describe wife inheritors, take even Apisy's poem and read it to him a hundred times, call him bewitched, Omogo was already caged in a way that set the villagers' tongues wagging. The foul smell from the bats that clung to the rafters of his roof sent him packing whenever he slept in his draughty hut back home.

Omogo wished he had discovered Akoko earlier, he could have nothing to discuss with his under-age girlfriend, who had assisted him to break *osuri*. The latter was juicier.

The boiled vegetable meals his mother prepared smelled like rotten onions to him, according to the new development.

Asem turned wild and, flanked by Akumba, braved her way to Akoko's home at midnight. Akoko, who heard their shouts from the gate, pried the door open. She was prepared for the worst.

"Please kill me but don't touch my husband! Kill me! Please kill me! But don't touch my husband!" Akoko's crackling voice rose above her attackers. The incident created another scene that was like a replay of Achola's unholy acts on her brother at the same time in the neighbouring home sometime back.

Akoko's home was soon crowded by bewildered spectators from neighbouring homes, including Akuota, who watched from a distance. Omogo, who had escaped through the window, was taking refuge at Akuota's kitchen courtesy of Achola in the neighbouring home.

Akoko ran to her husband's grave and shouted at Asem: "Here he is, resting in peace! Wake him up and tell him that I'm married to Omogo."

Akoko's acrobatics successfully scared away her enemies and spectators. She screamed in her compound the whole night, calling her late husband to wake up and save her from intruders.

Her public declaration gimmicks won the approval of community stakeholders who concluded that Ogoma, after all, had performed basic but not all the rituals required from an inheritor. She was free to pick a man of her choice.

Akoko's three children, Okodhe - a boy, Otiende - a boy and Asewe - a girl, were still too young to control their mother. All they could do was to watch helplessly. The eldest, Okodhe, was only thirteen years old.

They peeped through some slits in the reedy door of the hut built for Okodhe on the left-hand side of her main house, according to culture because he was illegitimate.

Asem's reaction was understandable to any parent who has a child, either a boy or a girl. Her son was not as lazy as other village louts. He had lots of skills in rural craft, and was the most sought-after service provider.

As much as he had used a young village bimbo to break the *osuri* of his hut, he had no family. She felt it wise for Omogo to start a family first and, maybe, go into wife inheritance later, just like Ogoma and Okong'o had done. Akondo's sprouting banana suckers adage would serve better in his case.

Asem feared for the future of her only son. Older women were notorious for bewitching their younger spouses. Their powerful magic blindfolded the boys and confined their senses of love to the older women's shackles.

"A boy immersed in widow inheritance menace will never admire any other girl! He's bewitched," Asem cursed.

"Leave him alone, Mama. Can you remember the night he wrestled me to the ground and ripped off my clothes? I feel he's better off when engaged to anything in skirt, even if it's a monkey in the name of a woman," Akumba complained with a careless wave of her hand.

CHAPTER SIXTEEN

Akoko, flanked by her new catch and Achola, joined the others in helping Aswayo, Osweta's first wife, whose health condition called for the intervention of community members. She stretched out her hand to greet Asem, who offered only the tips of her fingers, with her nose pointing the roof, instead of a full handshake; a clear indication of some harboured grudges.

Osweta's sofa set and other table chairs in the sitting room of his house were packed with visitors, comforting his first wife, laid on a mat at the centre of the floor. Akumba, seated next to the mat, offered a full handshake with a wholesome smile that encouraged Akoko to feel at home and participate like any other member of the community.

"Akoko, what happened between you and me?" Akondo, seated next to Akuom, asked.

"Why?" Akoko asked.

"You don't visit me nowadays."

"Just busy with my domestic chores," Akoko answered with a sigh of relief.

"It's too hot, why do you cover her with such a thick woolen blanket," Akoko complained, stooping low to lift the blanket from Aswayo.

"My bedsheet was chewed by a cow when I hanged it in the open to dry after washing," Osweta explained.

"I have a new one; you'll receive it tomorrow," Akoko offered.

"Can I send someone to come for it?" Osweta asked.

"Don't worry, I'll send my husband," Akoko's last word, 'husband', sparked negative reactions and cheers in equal proportions. The labour pain Asem had felt while delivering Omogo resurfaced. She gave Akoko one ugly look and left in a huff. Asem tumbled on Osweta's compound towards the gate with her feet flapping in the air like some two birds struggling to fly after swimming in a pool of *andiwo*. She mumbled toxic curses against the predator that whisked away a chick from her nest.

Akoko went ahead with the diagnosis, as if nothing had happened. She repurposed her hand into a thermometer and placed it on the chest of the patient to know her temperature. "Her temperature is too high," she complained.

She planted her knees on the floor to carry her body and stooped, placing her right ear close to Aswayo's chest to know her blood pressure. "Judging from the heart-beat, her blood pressure has gone higher," she complained.

She whispered to the patient's ear to test if she could utter a word, but Aswayo struggled to open her mouth, which seemed to have succumbed to locked jaws. Only some deep groan could be heard.

Akoko fought back an upsurge of tears in respect of the cultural restrictions against mourning a person before her death. She rose and sat back on her seat next to Omogo and whispered to Akuota's ears, with grief on her face: "Why didn't you tell me that it was such bad? Achola just informed me today."

"I've been too busy. I couldn't come to your place," Akuota answered.

"But you just send Ombwede, he's my regular customer."

"Sorry, I also got the message late when Ombwede was away," Akuota answered.

"Kindly let me know when you'll be coming for an overnight vigil. We can't leave her alone with her husband in this state."

"I'll let you know. I also fear walking alone at night," Akuota offered.

***

The two women chatted on their way to Osweta's home for an overnight vigil to help their elder, Aswayo, who was a few years older than Akuom. They ensured they served and released their customers before leaving.

176

"Don't tell me you left before serving supper to your husband," Akoko lamented.

"No, he's okay. He was already asleep by the time I left," Akuota assured.

"Mine ate and left for a village disco dance," Akoko said with a chuckle.

"Don't mind. He belongs to the young generation. He may quit if you become too strict," Akuota advised.

"In fact, he and your son, whose wife is already pregnant, went together."

"Even Achando has to be tolerant. Ombwede is not his age, but I'm glad he now understands love. He's not as bitter with me as he used to be," Akuota commented.

"Even Achola will calm down once she gets a serious lover. Leave alone irresponsible stone throwers who lure them for leisure and fly away," Akoko advised.

"But my daughter is pigheaded. She's too arrogant to maintain a husband," Akuota complained.

"It's the influence of alcohol, she'll change if she stops drinking," Akoko advised.

177

"Which magic can we use to stop her from excessive drinking?" Akuota asked.

"Visit Achwiya, she'll help you. Can you remember my late husband stopped drinking almost two years before his demise?" Akoko reminded.

"Thank you, I'll try," Akuota appreciated.

"What can I do to mend fences with Asem? She's too bitter about my relationship with her son," Akoko consulted.

"Bring a young girl of your blood and convince Omogo to marry her, your relationship will continue as you also help to bring up his family," Akuota advised.

"Does culture allow that?" Akoko asked curiously.

"Yes, say a daughter to your brother. The Luo culture allows her to marry even your legitimate husband," Akuota advised. "If you have any doubts, please visit Akondo for more advice. Culture also allows somebody to inherit his step mother. For instance, Okong'o would be allowed to inherit Akinyi, Aswayo's co-wife if Osweta died today."

The two women broke into sprinting and screaming on hearing a commotion that shook the fence adjacent to the footpath on which they were walking. They thought they had fallen into the trap of Ratila, only to realise that it was a rabbit in a trance. The rodent jumped out of its hideout on hearing their footsteps.

Akoko delivered a new bedsheet to Osweta and sat on a chair, followed by Akuota, who sat next to her. The number of caretakers had reduced to less than half the attendants found there in their day time visit, most of them aged community members, who had no interest in the village disco performing in a home across the stream, facing Okebe's new home.

"Thank you, daughter," Osweta appreciated.

Akondo and Onyoyo consulted in whispers on matters pertaining to the condition of their patient. They discussed at length the eerie sound of some crows heard cawing overhead in the same compound two days earlier. The birds known for sending bad signals when the angel of death was about to unhook somebody's soul drew attention of the two old men.

Aswayo's eyes sank inside, leaving only a pair of empty sockets, covered with some withered sunken eyelids, giving their final dragging blinks. She could no longer look at people straight in the eyes, a dangerous sign of preparations to join her ancestors.

The patient breathed with a croaking sound as if her chest was packed with dozens of frogs. Osweta was already moaning and sniffling in a cowardly fashion, like a scared prey. The hooting of an owl from atop a mango tree behind the fence of Osweta's home was an alarm for Aswayo's last moments on planet earth.

179

Okong'o, who had camped in the home for a number of days, sat on the chair next to the door, gritting his teeth with threats to clobber the witch suspect in case his mother died. Akinyi, Osweta's second wife, the suspected witch, sat quietly on the *branda* of Aswayo's house, her chin in her palms, to express sorrow and innocence.

A few minutes past midnight, Aswayo's whole body stretched on her mat dangerously, her fists coiling into a weapon, her eyes rolled round and stopped altogether, neither blinking nor rolling, she clamped her teeth together, heaved her chest and breathed out a lungful of hot air...! She breathed her...last! Aswayo was...gone! Gone to an unknown destination, she was...gone! Her tears stimulus lifeless body left back, on the floor, to the mercy of mourners, she was...gone! To no man's land, she was...gone!

Akondo and Onyoyo held Osweta in a firm grip to stop him from any crazy actions resulting from the loss of a woman who had lived with him for over fifty years. Akuom led the other women in straightening Aswayo's body and putting it in good order that'd look appealing to mourners.

Okong'o's temper went beyond control, prompting him to run up and down his father's compound, growling like a fighter bull. His sound elicited tears in frenzied mourners, who scampered to all corners of the

180

home wailing and acting variously to express condolence. Akinyi screamed loudest to expunge her name from the list of suspects behind Aswayo's death.

The home was soon crowded by mourners from all over the village. Akuom remembered the story of Akondo's deceased wife, the *ang'uola* issue, and insisted that Osweta had to be there when they were dressing the body.

Osweta, with his experience in cultural matters, didn't need an advisor but just people to condole with him. With order from Akuom, Osweta was given a cane to whip the body of his wife because throughout their marriage, he had never beaten the woman as stipulated in the traditional law that a woman must be beaten. A man who never beat his wife when she was alive must whip the body of his dead wife before funeral arrangements start.

"What a bad woman! Eh!" Osweta growled insincerely at the corpse while whipping it, his face bearing fake anger.

In a society where death was never natural, mourners wailed with questionable remarks targeting suspected killers although expressed in parables to dodge interrogations. Names of *ndagla* (killer plant) planters, transmitters of *sihoho* and the co-wife dominated the blame- list.

181

HIV test results, which were positive when Aswayo was tested while still alive, were never given consideration. Neither did they consider Aswayo's age to treat her case as death from natural causes.

Herds of cattle were brought to the home by relatives and friends to mourn the woman. They lined up and entered the house in style as if they had been trained on how to mourn a dead person. They entered the house one after the other, smelled the body in turns and made U-turns.

Grave diggers worked overnight on the eve of the burial day. Charged by Akuota's product bought for the same purpose, the young men had the rectangular six feet grave ready within six hours.

On the burial day, Osweta's home was cramped by mourners from all corners of their social networks. Okong'o's estranged wife, a great friend of her deceased mother-in-law, made a surprise entry to join mourners. Her children, thrilled by her presence, walked with her wherever she went. Okong'o feigned commitments to avoid the sight of the woman he didn't want to see walking freely and rejoicing together with mourners, who gave her a warm welcome. His inherited widow escaped through the fence to avoid public ridicule.

Huddled together at a secluded corner in a shroud of shrubs was a group of VUP mourners; Osweta's son-in-law and his entourage. Audi, the husband of one of Okong'o's younger siblings, was barred by cultural rules from entering the home of his wife's origin; he had never paid the ritual introductory visit to eat the sacred hen empowered to officiate his blood relationship with his in-laws. Unscrupulous entry before performing the marital ritual was a seed of disaster that would ruin his entire family.

Their skins got scorched by the heat of the sun while their colleagues who had performed the ritual relished VIP1 treatment in the cool breeze of shady places under trees inside the home. The VUPs, writhing in the scorching heat outside the home, were also not allowed by culture to eat anything solid. They were served drinks.

No son-in-law was allowed to join the mourners before the body was covered in a coffin, which was tantamount to seeing their mother-in-law naked.

Time for testimonies, the master of ceremonies called out names, one after the other.

"Josephine Akuom, please come forward and give your testimony," the MC called.

"Thank you. My name is Josapin Akuom," Akuom introduced herself. "My address is Parasis Akondo," she introduced herself amid giggles.

"This lady, whose body is resting in the coffin in front of me, is like my elder sister. I got married in this village when she already had three children. She contributed a lot to the nurturing of my family until I got established. I was a fan of music and could at times escape from my late husband's bed when the sound of music from a village disco filled the airwaves. I'd take refuge in her home when my habit provoked kicks and blows from the father of my children. May her soul rest in peace."

"Thank you, Josephine,'' the MC appreciated. "Next is the co-wife to the deceased; Jenipher Akinyi come over please."

"Thank you MC. Aswayo is like my elder sister. She and I have lived in peace since I got married to Osweta thirty years ago. We've never quarreled...." Argh!

Akinyi's last words sparked reactions expressed in grumble that forced a halt for a minute. It was an open lie. Her audience was aware of the constant wrangles with Aswayo over their man. The worst instance was the night Osweta almost killed her with a spear when she was caught eavesdropping, her ear positioned near Aswayo's bedroom window. Osweta picked up his spear from under the bed and popped out to kill, unaware that it was his wife out there. He lunged forward to kill either Ratila, the *piti-piti* man, or a thief; only to hear a screech from his second wife, pleading: "Don't kill me please! Am your wife!"

When elders, including Akondo, asked her about her business near somebody's bedroom window, she lied that she had gone there to look for

184

a jewel which she had lost two days earlier. She had indeed lost her jewel but it was a jewel in quotes, Osweta had spent two nights in Aswayo's house.

Akuom stood and advised her to ignore the grumble and speak on.

"OK, they said, don't poke your nose into the affairs of somebody's family while back home, your dogs are fed on vegetables and cows eat meat!" Akinyi's angry remarks evoked rowdy reactions from her audience, who threatened to leave if she couldn't stop at that point.

"May my sister's soul rest in peace," she concluded and sat back in protest.

"Next," the MC called "is Aswayo's eldest son, Okong'o."

"Thank you," said Okong'o. "My name is James Okong'o, the eldest son in this home." The voice was hoarse from two days of mourning.

"Apart from raising us," he went on, "she nurtured my first family until the devil separated us."

Like his step mother, Okong'o's false testimony sparked grumble from his audience, who knew well the cause of his wife's departure. He was the lazy type, walking from one den to another begging for *andiwo* and demanding for food from either his estranged wife or his mother. "Why tarnish the devil's name?" they asked.

185

For the sake of peace, Okong'o concluded his testimony and resumed his seat.

"Next is Adongo, Okong'o's legitimate wife," the MC called.

"Thank you. I am Mary Adongo," she said. "I was married in this home for some time. But I can't go into details because all of you know what I went through before giving up and returning to my home of origin."

"We know!" the crowd cheered up.

"This lady who has now left us has left a gap that'll never be filled. When I was here, although married to a man who was alive and healthy, I was like a widow. Why? Because I was the sole breadwinner, contrary to the norm of having a man as the provider for his family! Mama did a lot to help me sustain my family. Had it not been for her effort, I'd have left earlier. May her soul rest in peace," Adongo concluded.

"Next," the MC said, "is Aswayo's eldest daughter, Anjeline, who'll speak on behalf of all daughters."

"Thank you. I am the eldest daughter in this home. I'm married in Sakwa. Just to tell you about Mama, she was a mother and a friend. She protected us a lot in our childhood, mostly against our eldest brother, who used to knuckle-knock our heads, known popularly as *ngoto*." Anjeline's word 'ngoto' caused laughter.

186

"She taught us well how to live with people and that's why we've maintained our marital relationships up to now. May her soul rest in peace," Anjeline concluded.

"Finally,'' said the MC, "I'd like to call Aswayo's husband. Osweta, please come over and deliver your testimony."

Osweta waddled to the front, flanked by Onyoyo and Akondo with the aim of giving first aid in case he collapsed. His face resembled the leather from the cow slaughtered to feed mourners during the burial ceremony, probably because of the predicaments surrounding his wife's death. A group of choir people welcomed the old man with a song to strengthen his spirit.

"Thank you, my son. Aswayo has been with me for over fifty years as my wife. I met her in the pre-independence days when she visited a sister of hers, who was a wife to my neighbour in the staff quarters of a sisal plantation owned by a white man, our employer. She was a young, gorgeous lady who attracted masses in the same plantation, prompting me to fight with other men to secure her." He caused laughter as he trembled to force out words.

"Even at the time I was marrying my second wife, I had no problem with Aswayo. I did it to get sons, who would protect my family because Aswayo and I had only one son, who is a *'goi goi'*, worthless person, and

187

six daughters." Osweta turned his face to the left and beckoned to Adongo. "Come over, daughter. Come over please. Look! Just look at this beautiful girl. She left my home because of the burden she carried; what a big loss to this community!" Osweta praised his daughter-in-law.

"Give her to me; I want to marry her!" Pong' shouted from behind the tent.

"We lost two daughters, twins, and remained with four, who have done me proud because they're successfully married. With my second wife, I have three sons and a daughter. May her soul rest in peace." Osweta's audience applauded him as he concluded.

Okong'o left in a huff following his dad's remarks that amounted to public embarrassment as the ceremony continued.

"I am now handing over this ceremony to the preacher, who'll help us to lay our mother to rest," the MC announced, handing over the microphone to the preacher.

The choir played tambourines with their lovely songs to usher in their preacher.

"Mama is already dead, but I have a message to pass to the living!" the preacher announced, flipping through his bible.
"The Bible says: 'For God so loved the world! That He gave His only begotten son! For whoever believeth! Shall be saved! But he who resists!

Shall perish! That's the word of God and not me!" the preacher patted the back of his bible. He continued: "The end time is here with us! We have disasters that cannot be defined by the elders who know all about cultural rules that prevent chira! You tell them about AIDS, they twist it to chira! Their teachings are doomed! Believe, today, in the word that will set you free from the shackles of cultural rules! Rules that bind a widow to an inheritor! They wander from one home to another, inheriting widows and spreading HIV!"

"Yemina (amen)!" a fringe of believers in the crowd yelled.

"Jesus will set you free from the witchdoctor, who advises you to walk with a bone dangling from your waist! Jesus will set you free, from the shackles of tin owners of Ng'iya! My sister you go there looking for an inheritor! You kick a tin, somebody as ugly as a baboon emerges from nowhere, claiming to be your man! Receive Jeeesus!"

"Yeminaaah!" the believers yelled their support to the gospel.

"If you believe in Jesus and have enough faith, you don't need to go to the hospital! You'll be healed by faith!" the preacher roared.

The controversial preacher's words seemed to be stepping on the toes of the majority. This hard-hitting preacher must have colluded with some informer from around who advised him on where to aim his sword.

His words were blowing over to the kitchen where Akuota and Akoko were busy preparing meals for mourners. Cultural hardliners like Akondo felt embarrassed by his remarks but they couldn't pin down God's messenger.

Akoko and Akuota vented their spleens on mannerless children who stood near the meal tent to taunt selfish mourners serving themselves too much food. The kids waited by the entrance and sang birthday songs to mourners who scooped more than their stomachs could carry:

"Happy birthday to you. Happy birthday to you. Happy birthday to you you you, happy birthday to youuu..."

Akinyi generously sprinkled a sample of soil together with her husband on the grave of her co-wife to prove that she was clean on circumstances surrounding the death of the old woman.

Achwiya visited Osweta's home three days later and shaved the heads of all the members of the family in accordance with the custom, apart from Ouko, the born again Osweta's son with his second wife.

CHAPTER SEVENTEEN

Osweta had spent a whole week in the cold without a sweet dream from his late wife. He had no grudge against handlers of the body who forced him to join them as an observer when the body was being dressed. But something must have gone wrong between him and his wife in her last days.

Osweta's attempt to visit Achwiya for some counseling or treatment hit a snag when the traditional doctor screamed at the devil trying to enter her home with *okola*.

"Man! Don't enter my home with *okola*..!" Achwiya screeched. The herbalist grouched loudly about Osweta's lack of nous to stop him from entering people's homes with the filth of his deceased wife.

"He's too old to claim that he doesn't have the traditional notions of cleansing himself after the death of his wife!" she snarled.

Osweta waddled back to his home feeling his feet had metarmophosised into tyres of a trailer. They were too heavy to lift from the ground. He felt as if his heart was melting away like wax. He made a jerky halt with the support of his walking stick to respond to Akwede's greeting by the roadside.

"Kindly help me reach my home, daughter. I am running short of oxygen," he pleaded.

Akwede, who was on her way to the spring-well, hid her bucket in a thicket and held the octogenarian widower by his right hand to support him on his way back home.

By virtue of nature, Osweta was too old to have any romantic sweet dreams. He shivered from the effect of the chilly night wind that had blown over him for a whole week. He dragged his tired feet, with the support of Akwede, to a shade where he succumbed to a slumber on a seat.

"Old man! Old man!" Achwiya's breathy voice roused him.

"Welcome doctor," he said, his finger pointing at a seat in front of him.

"I am sorry for the embarrassment, but I hope you understand our culture," Achwiya, who had rushed over to restore Osweta's confidence apologised.

"Now, tell me. How did you want me to help you?" she asked.

"I've been in the cold for the last one week but I've not been able to meet my wife," Osweta complained.

"Lick this tonight after supper and spend another night in the cold. Her spirits are still hovering around here over some issues, but this will set you free," Achwiya explained and gave him some ash wrapped in a piece of paper.

"Thank you," Osweta appreciated, stretching forth his arms to receive the magic ash.

Osweta fell asleep at 11pm after dozing on his seat in the cold for two hours. His dream took dimension miles away from the world of romance.

A misty image of his grandchildren running up and down the compound, with cowdung on their palms, smearing the earthen wall of Aswayo's main house, came to him. He tried to shoo them away but they ridiculed him and cheerfully went ahead with their naughty behaviour. Adongo popped out of Akinyi's house to chase away the kids. She moved towards him and stooped to the level of his seat for a hug but Osweta woke up while trying to coil his arm round her neck as a response to the hug from his daughter-in-law.

"What a queer dream?" Osweta said to himself, wondering. In what was supposed to be his wife, came his daughter-in-law. She was like one of his children and the devil trying to drag her along his romantic line had to be rebuked.

9am local time, Achwiya was seated facing Osweta in his shade. A keen interpretation of his dream devalued his moral demeanour.

It depicted him as a spoilt old man with a whiff of some appetite for the young generation. Osweta's dream was successfully linked to the way he lifted Adongo's hand in public on the day of his wife's burial. There was public disquiet at the words he used to praise the estranged wife of his son and his gesture when he lifted her hand.

"Old man, your deceased wife has expressed her anger. The way you lifted Adongo's hand on the burial day and endearments was like empowering her to take Aswayo's place. Can you imagine?" Achwiya revealed.

Beads of sweat rolled down Osweta's cheeks, prompting him to cover his face in shame. He shed tears to demonstrate the level of frustration he experienced after learning that a member of the spirit world had such feelings against him. Her influence would even mobilise some forces from above to strike him with thunder.

"Just open up for me to help you, Osweta. Did you, at any one time, feel that Adongo had some space in your heart?" Achwiya asked, looking straight into his eyes.

"That's like one of my biological daughters! What are you trying to tell me?" Osweta retorted.

"Did Aswayo, at any one time, suspect you to have a relationship with another woman simply because you talked to the woman nicely or even smooched her?"

"Yes."

"Who is this woman and how?"

"Akwiri, Amami's mother. It was one month after burying Rabidhi." Osweta revealed.

"Why did she suspect you?"

"Because of my saucy jokes."

"But did you intend to inherit her?"

"No," Osweta lied.

Osweta knew Achwiya's antics of gleaning people's secrets while offering her services. She once ordered Achando before marrying Ombwede to shout out the name of Akula's biological father. The naïve single mother shouted out Swale's name three times before the medicine woman could offer her service. She claimed that the child got healed because Achando had unveiled the secret to her ancestors.

"It's the nature of any woman. Her spirits are as jealous in the other world as they were here," Achwiya explained.

"How do we go about it?" Osweta asked.

"Take this." Achwiya offered a bottle of greenish herbal solution.

"Drink half of it after supper and spray the rest on Aswayo's grave, then resume your sleep back in your house, OK?"

"Should I sleep in Aswayo's house or Akinyi's house?" Osweta asked.

"No! Not Akinyi's house. That'll sow dangerous seeds of disaster. Don't sleep in Akinyi's house before you cleanse yourself," Achwiya warned.

"How do I go about it?"

"Get a woman to cleanse you of your wife's filth before going to her rival's house," Achwiya advised.

"How?"

"Spend with her in Aswayo's house."

Osweta found himself in unfamiliar circumstances. Getting a woman at his age for cultural reasons was not an easy task. Which woman was ready to be used for such demeaning purposes? It's the same case with village girls used for breaking *osuri*! Cultural pawns? Too demeaning. Not easy, unless you clinch the desperate type who is free for all.

Akwiri, the woman he secretly assisted to perform the cultural rituals after her husband's death would suffice, but it hit a snag when she told him off.

"Not in Aswayo's house!" she snarled at Osweta, who had organised for a private meeting with her.

Akuota and Akoko were seasonal friends and enemies. Today, they are hurling insults at one another across the fence, tomorrow, you see them walking together whispering village gossip to one another. As vendors of the drink that charges brains to do unholy acts in the village, they formed the best outfit when it came to fixing harmful plans.

"We have a discussion at Osweta's place and would like you to join us," Akuota invited Nyachula - daughter of an island, a regular customer notorious for excessive drinking. The woman was about two decades younger than Osweta, although her skin was too leathery from the effects of excessive drinking.

10pm local time, Osweta's table flourished with a bowl of fried chicken and a jerrycan of *andiwo* waiting under the table for motivation after the meal. The VIP1 treatment accorded to Nyachula was a God given opportunity beyond her wildest dream. No serious discussion was aired as she had expected. No agenda, just stories of the latest subjects of gossip in the village.

Akuota and Akoko served themselves glasses half full to prove that the drink was clean and had no bad notion.

"Serve yourself, Nyachula! Serve yourself! No limits please, feel free and drink. Three more jerrycans are available as soon as we clear this!" Akoko said with a chuckle.

In a desperate bid to seize the rare opportunity, Nyachula gulped down a full glass of *andiwo* that sent her wits to the dogs. She yelled taunts at the two women who encouraged her to binge more on the grog. She lost balance and fell off the chair to the floor. Akuota and Akoko slammed the door shut and left in a hurry, laughing heartily.

***

A cloud of uncertainty hung over the safety of Osweta's son, Ouko, the first-born son in his second family. He had a wife but culture did not allow them to sleep together as a husband and wife before the eldest son Okong'o did. Okong'o had not been in good terms with his dad since the old man embarrassed him in public during the funeral.

Okong'o touched the ground with his belly to swear that he'd never drink at Akuota's place because she accommodated his estranged wife who was still hanging around the village days after attending the burial of her mother-in-law. Community support and the love for her children anchored Adongo to the village, forcing Okong'o to play hide and seek games from critics who frequently reprimanded him about the failure in his parental responsibilities. Akoko did not spare him either. She constantly reminded him to reinstate Adongo.

A close observation of Ouko's remarks revealed that he had done the worst before his elder half-brother, citing negative cultural beliefs that lacked focus. He rebelled against any treatment from cultural activists and insisted that he was safe in the name of Jesus, according to his faith. But the balding grey-haired doyens of culture pinched their noses with a cursing remark: "We'll wait and see!"

Okong'o's intercourse with his inherited wife who had hooked him up at her home was not recognised by culture. He had to perform the rituals in his home either with his wife or with any woman he could lure in his dad's style as long as he engaged her in his matrimonial house. His inherited widow had forced him to allow Achwiya to shave his head for fear of sowing seeds of disaster if she kept him with his cursed hair.

Okong'o's house was scruffy with cobwebs. He risked being displaced from his home if Adongo acted as Akwede had done. All she needed was to make any change to the house and launch it in his absence. It'd be assumed that a ghost man performed the rituals on his behalf. He'd be dead in that case if he joined Adongo in the same house later. As the mother of the children dominating the home, she had strong roots in the home and could not be stopped by anybody if she had decided.

Mischief-makers, Akuota and Akoko, the women most notorious for fixing bad plans, had a field day looking for alternatives to reinstate their beloved friend. Okong'o's home would be livelier in her presence.

With support from Okebe and the likes of Akondo, Okong'o met the shock of his life when he was roused from his jolly at the widow's place by a herdsman who informed him that his house had been demolished. He rushed to his home only to find Omogo digging holes to lay foundation for another more spacious house than the demolished one.

The forces on the ground guarding Adongo against confrontation by her husband were too powerful to stop. Okong'o's anger relapsed into moaning. He ignored the labourers who were gloating over his frustrations and sidled towards Okebe, seated on a heap of the rubbles of his demolished house to air his grievances.

"Why have you done this to me my brother even if I was wrong?" Okong'o complained.

"We want Adongo to take care of her family," Okebe responded in a light tone.

Okong'o knew the chink in his armour. The glint of grief on his face buoyed his enemies with the spirit of victory. They sang traditional war songs as the building of Adongo's new house progressed.

The community's decision to build a new house for Adongo was not just for cultural reasons but the demolished house had been in bad state. Termites had eaten a big chunk of the poles supporting the wall, leaving it to bend to one side, almost crumbling down.

Donations were given generously to pump a fresh breath of life to Okong'o's home. Okebe's decision to buy iron sheets for the house uplifted Adongo to a higher level than Okong'o's capacity.

Okong'o's children celebrated the return of their mother. They'd no longer depend on Akinyi, their step granny, who had taken care of them since their mother left the home swearing that she'd never return.

Akwede, although impressed by the new development, was worried why Akuota kept looking sideways while talking to her even when she talked to her freely to prove that she harboured no grudges. The condition imposed on Akuota by her witchdoctor was a prison of its own kind.

Okong'o vanished from his home like vapour. He was tired of sitting in his shade with no single sympathiser talking in his favour. But displacing a man from his home is not an easy task. He braved his way back late at night two days later to know who the man he was, that had a chest wide enough to inherit his wife before his demise.

Failure to receive any response after knocking his door several times prompted Okong'o to lower his tone to that of a beggar.

Adongo opened the door: "Come in but don't touch my body," she warned.

"Who do you expect to launch this house if not me?" Okong'o asked.

"What do you mean by 'launching'?" Adongo snarled.

"Why do you ask as if you're not a Luo?" Okong'o asked.

"Tell me what you mean by 'launching', dear!" Adongo asked, turning to Okong'o's side and looking straight into his eyes.

"OK, you pretend to be in darkness but you know very well that to establish a new house, you and I must spend together as is the custom," Okong'o explained.

"Spend with who? With you Okong'o? You? Over my dead body! All those rounds you've made inheriting women whose husbands died from AIDS related diseases! You expect me to-to-to...! A word deficiency syndrome ensued." The furious Adongo slammed the door shut and returned to her bed with a loud click of her tongue, leaving her man stranded in the sitting room with a tin lamp on the table to provide light that could enable him to see clearly the new development accomplished by her sympathisers.

The smell of fresh mud swirled around his nostrils. The glimmer of new iron sheets gave a new sparkling glint to his home in the bright moonlight. The villagers had done more than he himself could in his entire lifetime. Okong'o couldn't believe his eyes, seeing a new sofa set that had replaced some creaky wooden seats that used to be in his house, donated by Osweta, his dad when his demolished house was being built many years earlier.

No man would make such a sacrifice unless he had some fishy aim regarding his wife. It'd be a taboo if Okong'o made a mistake of spending a night in the house after a fellow man had spent in the same house on the first night of its launching. That would cause *chira* that was powerful enough to send him to join his mother in the spirit world. But judging from his wife's resistance and remarks, something fishy must have happened. Okong'o remembered Ogoma's case, and found himself in a sorry state.

Okong'o had thought of coming to his house the day the house was built but the ceremony went on until midnight. Akuru, his inherited widow, was also on his neck to ensure he did not spend in the house, purposely to own him permanently, like Akuota and Ogoma enjoying their sunset honeymoon without interference.

Okong'o gave a flinty glance at his bedroom, packed with a new four-by-six inches bed and mattress but he could not join his wife there for fear of *chira*. The man who funded all this development must have taken it a notch higher by being the owner of the home for that night.

"Okong'o! Okong'o!" Akuru's scratchy voice was heard calling across the fence.

"Go to your wife, she's calling you!" Adongo ordered.

Just like Akwede had a reason to love Akuota, Adongo had a reason to love Akuru. Those are the women who relieved them of the burden of lazy bones.

Akwede and Adongo were among the few who believed that AIDS is real and did their best to part ways with their unfaithful husbands. They cited examples of women like the late Akungu, who were submissive to their husbands even after learning that the men could not be trusted; they had succumbed to AIDS related infections, although cultural activists believed the couple died from *chira*.

"Why do you stick to a woman who has no business with you?" in a harsh whisper, Akuru asked Okong'o, who had crossed the fence to respond to her call.

"But that's my home!"

"Your home? Do you know the man who launched that house? You'll die like a dog if you're not careful! Man!" Akuru warned, with a careless wave of hands as they walked on the tortuous path towards her home in the bright moonlight.

"No man can sleep in my house before I die!" Okong'o retorted.

"Two whole nights after the house was built, you were away from that compound. Which magic wand did you shake to tell you about the occupants of your house? Try and sleep on the same bed for even a night, you'll face the wrath of our ancestors!" Akuru warned. "And get to know that that man called Okebe will never do anything just out of good heart."

Okong'o shivered on hearing the name of the man he feared. He felt more at home with Akuru than with Adongo. His own children behaved like Akwede's children did towards their dad; they no longer went to Akinyi's house when hungry.

Okong'o had no tangible evidence to prove that Okebe had snatched Adongo from him, but Okebe was the prime suspect because he had contributed generously to reinstate Adongo.

Arudhi, Akuru's only son and child, had no issues with Okong'o. The boy, on his 19th birthday, was well conversant with culture and understood love. He had since joined the stone throwers' club. Arudhi was notorious for exposing secrets concerning who was dating who. He exposed these on the leaves of sisal plants.

He once graffitised, in big capital letters: ADOYO DATES ARMSTRONG, a message that remained visible on the leaf of a sisal plant by the roadside for more than a fortnight before Achando alerted Adoyo, who went and angrily cut off the leaf. His stealthy way of doing it, mostly at night, kept him safe from the wrath of the offended.

A broken pot on the steeple of Akuru's grass thatched house was not for fun. The decision to place it there had been reached after a series of consultations with the village elders, who had been opposed to the marriage between Akuru and her legitimate husband, the late Swale. The two had some blood relationship that barred them from any romantic relationship, worst, marriage. Their mothers belonged to the same clan.

Powerful talons of blind love broke the barriers eons before, when Swale was still a teenager, active in the stone throwing exercise. He would sneak out at night and walk for miles to throw his stones on the roof of the kitchen where Akuru used to sleep with her peers, take her to his hut in his dad's home and escort her back in the wee hours of the following day.

The elders who had an inkling about their relationship ignored them as teenagers learning to exercise love, only to learn with a shock that the girl was pregnant. Swale's thirst for his baby created an unbreakable umbilical cord that tied him to the girl who soon joined him in the hut as the legitimate wife. The veil of secrecy surrounding Akuru's failure to deliver more babies revolved around the blood relationship and failure of the family to consult experts for solutions.

Call him rich or strong in terms of fist fights, Okong'o had to pursue a vendetta against Okebe. No man in this world, no matter how weak, can breathe with ease when a man like him, with the hallmark of manhood that equals his, steals the soul of his wife.

Ogoma's case was different. The man in his house was invisible. Just spoken about in hushed tones but no man came out in public the way Okebe did. Akwede had built her house using the merry go round proceeds from her women group. His advisor used the expression just in case a man sneaked in and performed the mandatory cultural ritual, he'd die from *chira* if he followed his rival's back, but there was no evidence at hand.

Okong'o thought of lurking around Okebe's gate with his panga and beheading him but memories of the day Okebe's iron fist crushed him like a fly held him back. Akuru noticed Okong'o's misery and advised him accordingly.

"If you want to send the man to his early grave, try and share a plate with him in a feast. That'll kill him faster if at all he's committed any adulterous act with your wife."

Okong'o appreciated Akuru's advice backed by experienced cultural activists who hated Okebe.

The begging bud that had infected Okong'o would not allow him to live as a permanent enemy of Okebe, who could offer him drinks in the village joints. He found the condition unbearable even on the dog days when he was sulking at Akuota for hosting Adongo.

Akuru had no capacity to quench his thirst for *andiwo* with her basket business. She'd buy expensive food but not drinks. Occasionally she'd give him only a few coins for his drinks but not to his satisfaction.

Akuru, who was also Akuota's regular customer, could share her glass with her inheritor in case they went together, mostly at Akuota's den where their love conversations started.

6pm local time, Okong'o sat enjoying the cool breeze of the evening behind Akuru's house after relishing a plate of fried eggs. Arudhi, his 'son', was busy trimming the fence of the home. His throat was too dry to wait for Akuru, who had gone to the market to sell her woven baskets and probably buy some food for supper using proceeds from the basket business.

A group of villagers trekking on the path across the fence were going to Akuota's den. Okebe's sound was heard clearly rising above the clamour. Okong'o lost his wits and crossed the fence at a high gear to catch up with his cronies. The stiff-necked Okebe jabbered on as if nobody had joined them even when Okong'o outstretched his hand for greeting.

"Yes, thank you," Okebe responded to Okong'o's greeting, his nose pointing the sky, his right hand coiled and pocketed to snub Okong'o's desperate hand.

Okong'o made two steps backward and greeted Omogo and Ratila to shade the embarrassment. He sat last on the bench at Akuota's den in a word deficiency situation. Akuota placed empty glasses in front of her customers without discrimination.

"Give them two *ondagos* each," Okebe ordered.

Okong'o rued the day he contemplated Okebe's murder. The village tycoon placed orders without discrimination.

The second round of his order that added three more *ondagos* of the grog to every glass burst riverbanks of words from the mouths of his disciples. Okong'o was not aware that he had been a subject of discussion before and after Adongo's house was built.

"Okebe you're worth being a leader of this community! Don't behave like some people who wait for other men to build houses for their wives!" Achola who had gulped down beyond her gauge yelled.

"Achola! Achola, can you listen to me? Please, daughter, can you listen to me?" Akuota pleaded with her daughter who ignored her and yelled even louder.

"No, Mama! If those are the kinds of men who must marry me, then I'll die unmarried!"

Achola's remarks triggered a barrage of insults that prompted Okong'o to react in defence.

"Look for a man! You're too old for your mother's home! Your younger brother is already married!"

Achando countered Okong'o by shouting from in front of her hut: "Stop using my husband's name as a scapegoat! Have you ever seen him wandering from one den to another begging for alcohol? Look here! Man! I don't drink *andiwo*, and don't try to drag my name to your bench of drunkards, OK?"

Achando's reaction was punctuated by several clicks of tongue to express anger. Ratila and Omogo were too drunk to speak out anything that would make sense. They sat with their weary faces stooped to the level of the table, just slurring words in support of fighting opponents. All they said was "Yeeesh-yesh…", without caring what they were supporting as they tried to raise their tired eyes to look up.

Achola's ears were too keen on what Okong'o was muttering to himself in a low tone with his head bowed.

"*Hududu fuong'!* You bewitched a man many years your junior to marry you," Okong'o muttered.

"Achando, can you hear what this goat is trying to say?" Achola shouted.

"What?" Achando popped out of her hut with her hands on her waist, her forehead crinkled up into a warrior, to hear from Achola.

"Okong'o is saying that you bewitched Ombwede to marry you! And he's calling you *hududu fuong*'"

"What about you? Lazybones! Were you the type to marry a woman as beautiful as Adongo? This lout…!" Achando barked.

She lunged forward and yanked Okong'o by the waist, hefted him from the bench and flung him to the ground with a force that scared away all the customers. Okong'o's feet knocked the table with a force that splashed off the dregs of *andiwo* left at the bottom of the glasses onto the table.

Sprawled on the ground facing the sky with a pregnant woman atop his chest, showering his face with girlish blows was Osweta's eldest son, flailing his hands desperately and kicking the air like a dying horse, sweating profusely and trying his weak blows against the electric muscles of Ombwede's catch, intestinal gases burbling down his bowels out into the air.

Akuota rushed to the scene and wrested her daughter-in-law from Okong'o. None of the customers was willing to separate them. They just

211

enjoyed the fight, raising their drunken faces and giggling in a drunken stupor.

Achola was already cracking her ribs with laughter in front of their kitchen, seated at the same spot where Akuru had been seated the day Okong'o started sending love signals to her.

"Leave me alone, Mama! I must beat this idiot! Leave me alone!"

Achando struggled to wrest her arm from Akuota's grip.

"Look! Fighting with a man in this state will afflict your child with *chira*," Akuota whispered to Achando's ear.

"He needs to trim his words! I'm not a drunkard like he is!" Achando muttered with a resignation and walked back to her hut, puffing and panting.

Naughty grins followed Okong'o's back as he staggered towards the gate. Akuota, who was not impressed by the incident, wore a donkey face. She left her customers under the care of Achola and crossed the fence over to Akoko's home where she found Ombwede seated with other customers irrigating their throats with glasses of *andiwo*. She waved at them and beckoned to Akoko for some private discussion.

"Kindly advise this boy on my behalf," Akuota requested.

"Why?" Akoko asked suspiciously.

"His wife has committed a sacrilege."

"What has she done?" Akoko asked curiously.

"Imagine, she fights with men in her state," Akuota said.

"Please, tell me what has happened. I know she doesn't drink," Akoko requested with a scared look.

"Okebe and his entourage came to my home, your man amongst them, for evening drinks. Achando started a fight with Okong'o in a feud perpetrated by Achola," Akuota explained.

"How did this happen?" Akoko asked, moving closer and listening more keenly.

"Achola was involved in a word tussle with Okong'o, who, by mistake, reminded her to look for a man, citing her younger brother's marital status. My daughter-in-law, irked by the inclusion of her family, lunged forward and perilously flung Okong'o to the ground with kicks and blows," Akuota narrated.

"What?" Akoko screeched, hands clamped behind her head. "*Mayooh-mayo-mayo!* And where is Okong'o by now?"

"He's gone back to Akuru's place."

"Do this; let me advise Ombwede before he leaves this place to take action. Such a woman deserves beating. Even we, if you can remember, were beaten by our husbands to become good women. But a woman given such freedom will keep on straying until one day you'll be shocked to see

213

her committing unholy acts like Achola's. Even Achola could have been a good girl if there had been an elder brother to discipline her with some strokes whenever she strayed," Akoko offered.

Akoko saw Akuota off and beckoned to Ombwede, leading him to a secluded place.

"Don't tell me that my wife has given birth," Ombwede said with a chuckle because he had noticed his mother discussing something sensitive with Akoko.

"Which birth? Is your wife a goat to carry a baby for five months in gestation?" Akoko responded with a smile.

"I just want to give you a report and then advise you accordingly," Akoko said.

"What happened?" Ombwede asked with a worried look.

"Achando has beaten Okong'o," Akoko reported.

"*Choke!* How did it happen?" Ombwede asked, shocked.

"Okong'o and Achola were quarrelling, and Okong'o referred to your family during the word tussle," Akoko explained.

"But she's right, how can Okong'o drag my family to an issue we don't know?" Ombwede supported.

214

"She may be right but culturally, a woman, especially a pregnant one, is not allowed to do such a barbarous thing to a man, no matter how weak or worthless the man is. It may harm your unborn baby."

The last words 'harm your unborn baby' irritated the worms in Ombwede's stomach. He stooped with his hands firmly clutched to his belly to contain ferocious worms screaming angrily—*njululu-njululu…!*

"A seed from my waist that I long to see…?" Ombwede screeched.

"What do you suggest?" he asked, prepared for action.

"You know what our culture stipulates. To bring sanity to your family, to cut the woman to size, to bring her down to a disciplined wife…! The woman must be beaten. You know how your father lived with your mother. You know how I lived with my husband. We were not good women but beating made us who we are today. We've managed to maintain our families even after the death of our husbands because we were beaten.

I can remember crossing the fence several times to save your mother from the wrath of your father. Even she, rushed to save me one night when my man was showering my back with strokes. That doesn't mean you hate your wife; culture should be preserved," Akoko advised.

215

Akoko offered two more *ondagos* to electrify Ombwede's brain for action and released him. He left at a high gear for action and ignored Omogo, who was lying unconscious near the fence of Akoko's home. He wormed through a hole in Akoko's fence and made his way to his hut armed with three canes from a guava tree.

The bang on the door of Achando's hut compelled her to squash into the small space under her squeaky spring-bed but Ombwede kicked the door open before she could fix herself, huge chunks of her thighs still trying to get a cover-up in the limited shadow under the bed.

Torturous strokes raining on her thighs smoked Achando out. She knocked Ombwede down and engaged him in a race that ended up at Akondo's home right inside the kitchen used by the beauties.

The hapless young woman found herself in the wrong hands when the occupants of the kitchen fled, leaving her to sort it out with her man. Ombwede's anger, stimulated by the force Achando used to knock him down went beyond control.

"Do you think I am Okong'o? Achando do you think I'm Okong'o?"

Ombwede's questions were punctuated by hot slaps on Achando's cheeks.

"Adoyo heeelp! Old man heeelp! Mama Akuom heeelp!"

Achando's plea for help would not succeed in a society where a man was saluted for beating his wife.

The bevy of beauties watching from outside had enough strength to coil Ombwede like a ball, pack him in a sack like a swag, load him onto their backs and take him to his hut. But they just watched from outside, lauding what the young husband was doing to his wife. A proof of his ability to control his women-folk.

Akondo sat in front of his *duol,* crackling cheeky giggles with his Akuom.

"My lord, don't kill me. I'm your wiiife! My lord, I can't fight you I'm your wiiife!"

This kind of plea glorifying Ombwede's superiority inflated his ego with a pugnacious spirit that infused more power to his fist.

Adoyo, whose way of handling issues was influenced by her own principles, felt an upsurge of anger soaring up in her throat and burning her chest, around her heart. She pounced on Ombwede with a force that flung both of them to the ground, giving Achando a way out to Akondo's vacated main house-cum-cereal store.

"Do you think you're a demigod? I'll prove to you today that you're not what you think you are!"

Adoyo trounced Ombwede with such remarks to restore sanity in the male dominated world ruled by a belief that every woman deserves beatings. Her peers wrested her from Ombwede's chest with warnings on the consequences of fighting with men.

CHAPTER EIGHTEEN

All roads led to Osweta's home one year after the demise of his wife. Lots of developments had happened in the village, both positive and negative. Ombwede and Achando were celebrating a gift from God: a healthy bouncing baby boy, whom they had christened Othiwi.

Many thanks to Armstrong whose records on Achando's HIV status during pregnancy had guided the healthcare professionals at the dispensary on how to administer HIV medicines to her. Contrary to her fear that she'd be subjected to a scheduled delivery through cesarean section, she had been diagnosed as having undetectable viral load at the time of delivery hence allowed to have a natural child delivery. Baby Othiwi's HIV results were negative. Achando maintained a strict observation of the counselor's advice to exclusively breastfeed the baby for six months while taking her treatment.

Unlike Akula whose bushy eyebrows, chocolate-brown skin and flat pan-cake shaped head with curled scattered hair reminded everybody of the late Swale, Othiwi donned a striking resemblance to Ombwede - chubby cheeks, a pair of dimples that formed whenever he smiled and wobbly lips that also characterised the late Odhialo's mouth.

But just a pitfall in their joy; Ombwede was ailing. His flickering health condition engaged the community stakeholders in endless battle with *chira*, whose source could not be traced. The health condition although sad but impacted positively on Achando's battle with HIV. His sexual frequencies had reduced drastically, inhibiting further re-infection from a rebellious husband who had rejected the use of HIV drugs, condoms and abstinence.

Adoyo was already married to the anti-AIDS crusader who had saturated the village with teachings against believing that HIV is a type of *chira*. They lived a happy life in a rented terraced house at a shopping centre two markets away from Akondo's home. The activist, known by his first name, Armstrong, continued with his door to door visits in the village.

Akondo barred him from entering his (Akondo's) homestead because he had not gone there officially to eat the sacred hen that is mandatory for a son-in-law to officiate their marriage.

But at least Akondo felt relieved to see off the daughter who had been breathing down his neck as if she didn't understand the luster of love and culture. She proved to be human by accepting marriage as part of life.

The young family accepted Apisy as part of them. They lived with her, giving her all the necessary support.

Akondo felt more impressed when he learnt that the new glow on Adoyo's skin and extra-ordinarily huge body was a sign of his grandchild under manufacture in her womb. She looked like a spoilt angel expelled from heaven.

Villagers thronged Osweta's home to welcome the guest, Audi, the very man who had sweltered in the midday heat on the burial day. Aswayo's grave was covered with a white bedsheet, to stop Audi from seeing his mother-in-law 'naked', according to the custom.

It was a big day, both for the hosts and for Audi, the day of breaking the block that barred him from entering that home on the day he attended the burial of his mother-in-law. This was the day he'd start getting VIP 1 treatment.

The weather was calm and charming. Audi's wife, Amondi, had come home two days earlier to prepare the ground for her husband's big day. The late Aswayo's house was well prepared for her son-in- law's visit. Maidens from around had jointly plastered the wall and floor of the house with mud baked using a special type of soil only available at Rachwi, miles away from Osweta's home.

They applied their God given skills to draw beautiful flowers on the wall using ochre fetched from Uhembo. The one from Rachwi was grayish in colour, only recommended for use as a first coat before drawing flowers.

Aswayo's kitchen spewed out plumes of smoke that attracted Pong', the man with the strongest sense of smell in the entire village. He was notorious for feigning humility when hungry but was mischievous after filling his stomach.

"Kindly don't shame us in the presence of our visitors," Adoyo pleaded.

"I won't do it sister. I'll be mum throughout. I respect Audi and Armstrong," Pong' lied.

Three hens lost their lives to prepare the ground for Audi's big day. Akuom, seated on a stool in the kitchen was busy advising cooks on how to cut the sacred hen killed for Audi's bowl. She warned them against breaking it into smaller parts like the others cooked for ordinary purposes. Entrails had no place in Audi's bowl; these were reserved for the likes of Pong' and kids. The other parts of the sacred hen were left whole as stipulated by cultural laws.

Akondo's group of elders, seated in a shade under a mango tree near Akinyi's house had no business but just to grace the occasion. Clad in their ceremonial plumed caps and regalia, they discussed historical events and narrated Amondi's development from the day she was born, her

222

engagement and marriage, to the day such an important guest was coming home to her honour.

Rays of light from the cloudless blue sky shone on a group of visitors clad in swanky suits and official dresses as the sun rose towards the sky centre. Seven men and five women making keen steps from the gate of Osweta's home towards Aswayo's house invoked her spirits, prompting her to rejoice and dance on the stainless sheet covering her grave, as proved by the flapping of the sheet against the four stones pinning every corner to the grave soil.

The group of female hosts ululating and gyrating weirdly to the tune of traditional songs tickled Aswayo to express her joy in the chirping of the birds atop trees and even the baying of dogs, with their noses pointing the sky, as if thanking Amondi's creator for the big day, the day of shifting Audi from the VUP club to VIP 1 club.

Non-participants in the dancing activity stood aside, pointing fingers and consulting in hushed tones to know who amongst the seven men was the VIP 1.

"The one at the centre, flanked by three guys on both sides wearing suits of the same colour and design, followed by five women," Adoyo explained to Akumba who was gawping nervously at the guests.

A black handsome man with a formidable smile, towering above all the others, walking with a stoop, glistening black thick African skin, with hulking stainless white teeth glowing beneath two well chiseled chubby lips, that's he.

Audi looked gentle and calm in his way of handling issues from the judgment of close observers. This was apparent in the kind of life Amondi enjoyed, free from wife battery. She had never run back home with injuries inflicted by Audi, unlike most married ladies around. If there had been anything related to beatings, it must have been some light slaps once in a while to meet customary demands.

Maidens whispered their comments with a veil of 'lust' and envy in their remarks. Some naughty eyes flickered on the faces of the six guests who accompanied Audi as Akuom recited her prayers, all eyes closed, reason; if any of you is a bachelor, please look here! We exist! Unmarried!

Amen! All bums on the seats to mark the end of Akuom's prayer. A word of introduction from the visitors and hosts followed. Akuom, with the load of too much village on her chest, had totally failed to train her lips on pronunciation of her and her inheritor's first names, to the extent of pronouncing her own name like a native of a village where people scamper to safety at the sight of a car. Heads stooped when she rose to introduce herself.

"My name is Josapin Akuom, my address is Parasis Akondo," Akuom introduced herself, amid suppressed laughter.

But the maidens spoke with fabricated accent of South Nyanza Luo. They made their vowels longer than the Alego type to add luster to their tones. Clad in their best fashion, they served the visitors' tea laced with bread, groundnuts and entertainment, cracking jokes and laughing. The quality of tea prepared for Audi and his entourage was slightly better than the milky one Ogoma enjoyed daily at Akuota's place.

Ordinary folk, apart from teenage girls, on grounds of principles, were advised to keep off the visitors' sight after introduction to create an atmosphere conducive for freer socialisation.

Two of the six men who accompanied Audi were unfit for public consumption. They looked almost the age of Akondo. Service girls bowed at their words in awe to demonstrate discipline. With the other four who looked young and out for grabs, however, they swapped jokes.

A challenge in the introduction style of the guests was the failure to declare their marital statuses, which left the maidens hanging in the balance.

But Pong'...! Pong', with his madness after taking tea and devouring the entrails of the hen given generously to gag his madness, ambled over and stood behind Osweta's home, shouting in a voice that spoilt the party in the house occupied by guests: "Our dear visitors! Marry those girls! They are looking for husbands! We're tired of village men throwing dozens of stones to the roofs of our kitchens every night!"

His words hit the floor of the house like a ballistic missile. The damsels felt as though a whirlwind from the devil had stripped them naked.

Pong' proved to Okebe and Okong'o, who tried to chase after him for some flogging, that the springs in his feet were better than theirs. He barreled through the shrubs making zigzag movements that left his pursuers confused and frustrated.

"I hope you'll understand; every village must have a mad man." Akumba, holding a bottle opener said, chuckling and stooping to open the soda in front of the chief guest.

Time for late lunch, a trail of beauties carrying bowls of delicacies entered the house, one after the other. Audi's bowl of the sacred hen was carried by Akelo, under strict instructions from Akuom as to how to handle the delicate meal. The part of the hen earmarked for crashing by

Audi's hulky teeth would break barricades that had kept him behind walls for eons.

A cow tethered to a peg at the centre of the compound was not worth the dowry for a girl like Amondi, who had maintained an excellent rapport with her husband since they got married almost a decade earlier. It was for *ayie*, appreciation to her parents for having a girl with such a good record. Real dowry would be organised later.

The boys who goaded the cow to Osweta's home had arrived earlier, about an hour ahead of the guests. They had left in a rush after eating some second-class meals served by Adoyo's group.

The service girls quit the house after washing the hands of the guests to pave way for freer consumption, shy guests were notorious for losing appetite in the presence of hosts. Their throats would shrink hence the risk of getting choked while forcing down half-chewed food. They ate quietly and respectfully, all table manners observed, occasionally lifting heads to steal glances at Amondi's childhood photos that graced the wall of her parents' house.

Thank God, Pong' never noticed Audi's jumbo-sized teeth; he could have shouted a nasty insult with the weight that could crash down the ceremony to nuts.

The service girls jealously whispered irksome remarks about the size of Audi's teeth in the interlude of rest out of Amondi's earshot. Although stainless white and well shaped, they could be repurposed into spades if, by bad luck, Audi lost them in an accident.

All eyes were cast on the guests as they sauntered towards the gate to organise rewards for their hosts. They stopped at the same place where Audi had desperately stood with his entourage the day he attended Aswayo's burial.

Audi dug out a wad of one thousand Kenya shillings notes from his pocket to divide them according to the number of hosts to be rewarded. One of the two old men gave him a number of envelopes with the names of beneficiaries written on each.

"The first envelope belongs to Amondi's father and his brothers," the old man, who had introduced himself as Audi's uncle, advised.

Audi filled the envelope with three one thousand Kenya shilling notes and gave it back to him.

"The second envelope belongs to her step-mother and co-wives," the old man advised Audi, who filled it with three one thousand Kenya shilling notes and gave it back.

"The third envelope belongs to her brothers and male cousins," he proceeded. Audi placed in it a one thousand Kenya shilling note and gave it back to him.

"The third envelope belongs to her sisters and female cousins," he said. Audi placed in there a one thousand Kenya shilling note and handed it back to him.

"Last but not least, is the kitchen staff," he advised Audi, who filled it with a thousand Kenya shilling note and gave it back to him.

The guests ambled back to Osweta's home with rewards squashed to the old man's coat pocket. They resettled on their seats, which had been swabbed clean by the service girls. They summoned the hosts to the house for the last word before departure.

The bottle of *andiwo* on Okong'o's hand did not infiltrate into the hallowed floor by mistake. It was in compliance with custom to reward the guests with some *andiwo* purposely to intoxicate them and cajole any of them into revealing a secret he knew about the chief guest. A drunken guest could easily reveal if the son-in-law was a night-runner, like Ratila, or a chicken thief, back in their village.

"Just before you reward us, your brother-in-law has some gift to clear your throats for better intonation," Onyoyo said with a chuckle as

Okong'o handed over the grog to one of the youthful guests. Akumba distributed glasses to them and sat back.

As the saying goes, every village must have a mad man. One of the youthful guests seated near Audi filled his glass with *andiwo* while the others just dripped spoonfuls to invoke culture. He gulped down the drink and reclined on the seat.

The repressed guests controlled their anger as the custodian of rewards delivered a vote of thanks on behalf of Audi, who was not allowed to talk on his big day. He called out names of the beneficiaries and distributed the enveloped cash.

"This envelope belongs to the father and uncles," he said.
Onyoyo stood up to receive the reward on behalf of Osweta as the old man called out the respective beneficiaries.

"The second envelope is for the mother and step-mothers." Akinyi sprang up and received the reward.

"The third envelope is for brothers and male cousins." Okong'o received the reward on behalf of the mentioned beneficiaries.

"The fourth envelope is for sisters and female cousins." Anjeline received the reward on behalf of the mentioned.

"Last but not least, we have an envelope for the kitchen staff."

Achando moved forward and received the envelope on behalf of the kitchen staff.

The drunken guest seemed to have some good poise. He wriggled on his seat as if his pant had been invaded by an army of fire ants.

Only damsels were allowed to escort the guests on their way out to as far as they could go, reason: for them to create a network for further development, preferably romantic.

The two elderly guests took a different lane on the other side of the dirt road to pave way for freer discussions among the youthful male guests and the host ladies. The women who had accompanied the guests walked by their side at close range to help in convincing their equal gender in case of need. The elders pretended to be busy with their own discussions but stole glances at the youths to monitor progress.

The drunken guest straggled far behind his colleagues as if he wasn't in their group. Achola, who noticed him, slackened her pace to keep him company.

"You see this man married to your cousin," he whispered to Achola, pointing finger at Audi.

"Yes, tell me please," Achola whispered back.

"His dad is a *piti-piti* man," the man revealed in a harsh whisper, head bowed to hide his face.

231

"Serious!" Achola exclaimed.

"Yes! Back in our village we don't sleep at night. The father owns a snake almost six feet long. The serpent that wears expensive earrings bought from Ng'iya populous market accompanies him whenever he goes to bewitch people at night. The old man refused to accompany us because he feared we'd reveal that! None of my business!" the drunkard said, twisting his nose with pride.

"Thank you, my brother, for revealing this to me,'' Achola appreciated but sensed a lie in the queer story of a snake endowed with pinnas to hang earings. "We'll pray to God to protect my cousin from that witchcraft.''

"Do this please," the drunkard requested, "I'm looking for a girl to marry."

Something kicked in Achola's womb like a healthy baby in gestation. A flash of beckoning opportunity tickled her armpits.

"OK I'm single but still ambivalent about marriage," she responded, her voice full of sarcasm.

"No, please,'' he said. "Just organise and come to Audi's home in the guise of visiting your cousin. I'll pick you up from there as soon as I get wind of your presence. They're our neighbours," the drunkard pleaded.

"It's okay. I'll do that before the end of this season," Achola assented, her neck bending in the style of a smitten village girl.

They caught up with the leading group that had stopped by the roadside to wait for a public service vehicle. Baby Othiwi's scream for breast milk all through from home to the bus stage was godsend, to stop Achando from disturbing the single and bachelors in their discussions; she at least had somebody in the name of a husband, even though sickling. Her colleagues were not comfortable and wondered why she insisted on escorting the guests. Married young women, such as Adoyo and Adongo, in their wisdom said bye-bye to the guests at the gate and went back home.

It was time for hosts to celebrate after seeing off their guests. The cash reward was portioned out among them without brawl.

People ate and drank together, Adongo chatting happily and freely with her displaced husband. Okebe deliberately ordered Okong'o to eat with him from the same bowl, a decision that proved to the wife inheritor that he had no secret affairs with Adongo.

A word tussle ensued in Ouko's house between him and his wife, forcing Adoyo to intervene, but only to learn that the woman had shushed her child by taunting Ouko's brother-in-law by saying "I'll call Audi to bite you with his big teeth if you cry here!"

***

Wah! Every day is not a holiday! Folks, back to your work, face the realities of life a day after Audi's big day that came with lots of freebies.

Lazybones coiled back their tails and took covers under the wings of their inherited widows but...! Something sinister was blowing across the village that required divine intervention.

The rash of premature deaths called for an impromptu research on the new type of *chira* that was sweeping teenagers to their early graves hence robbing the community of the young generation, the wellspring of manpower and continuity. A big number of teenagers in their prime had been swallowed by the soil in the last one year not only in Nyakonja village but also in neighbouring ones and beyond. They were sobbing from the pain of losing the fathers and mothers of tomorrow, leaders of tomorrow and drunkards of today.

Ogoma's tinge of wisdom in his laziness had advised him to accept and use HIV drugs alongside *chira* antidotes and magic, like the pig-bone dangling from the string tied round Akuota's waist line. Obstinate believers in *chira*, such as Ombwede, scoffed at Armstrong and invested in Achwiya's solutions.

CHAPTER NINETEEN

All blames on Achola as Ombwede's skin developed rashes. His lips had cracks that tore the skin to an open wound. The taps of his bowels broke loose and paved way for diarrhea that kept jetting out as if he had a waterfall in his stomach. He was scrawny and crabby. His face developed wrinkles like one of the village octogenarians.

Ombwede vented his spleen on Achola, the girl he was made to believe was behind his *chira*, stemming back to the midnight incident when she had worked on him like a witch.

Achola's world narrowed to a cage. She was the punching bag of Ombwede's sympathisers. She was on the receiving end of threats, hate speeches, insults and all kinds of reactions you can imagine. Herbalists prescribed solutions with strict conditions on how to involve the suspect in treating the victim of *chira*.

Achwiya's herbal solution, delivered to Akuota in a five litre jerrycan, had to be mixed with half a glass of Achola's urine and given to Ombwede to drink one glass per day for a whole week.

Another herbalist from the far end of Alego provided some ash wrapped in a polythene paper with instructions that Achola had to spit on it every evening before giving it to Ombwede to lick.

Achola was traumatised by the belief that she was the witch killing her own brother. She imagined a situation of a widowed Achando plus her orphaned sons, all in her name and felt like digging her own grave and burying herself alive.

"His spirits will follow you wherever you go!" Pong' shouted at Achola on her way to the spring-well for a bucket of water.

Achola cajoled Akuom into giving her the direction to Audi's home, more than twenty miles away. She disappeared at cock crow the following day. Having no means of transport, she trekked until her feet developed elephantiasis! Worn out with the long-distance walk, she begged for a cup of water from an attendant in an eatery located at a shopping centre where Audi's family used to go for their recreations.

"Aunt! How are you Aunt Achola?"

Achola was shocked by a young excited girl, almost four years Apisy's junior, in such a far place who endeared her with her middle name.

"Aunt! Please let's go home," the child requested. "Where are aunts Achando and Amami?"

Achola was agile enough to conclude that the child was Amondi's eldest daughter, sent to buy a packet of salt, carried in her right hand.

"I've left them at home, they'll come tomorrow," Achola answered.

Amondi sprinted to the gate at the sight of Achola and gave her an overwhelming hug that restored her hope.

"What happened, cousin? You look so tired!" a trickle of tears rolled down Achola's cheeks as she struggled to narrate her ordeal.

"Just relax, cousin! Please don't cry!" Amondi pleaded.

She prepared some tea for her visitor and gave her warm water for bathing to get the tire out of her. Amondi organised for a meeting with Achola in a separate room to listen to her sob story.

Amondi expreseed her sympathy at the situation. One of the few who believed that AIDS is real, and encouraged people to go for VCT and use HIV medicines if found positive, she welcomed Achola to stay with her for as long as she could.

"Ombwede will die from AIDS related diseases if he can't renunciate *chira*," Amondi commented.

Two days in a foreign land after recuperating, Achola remembered her drunken boyfriend. She consulted Amondi with fear of rejection of the proposal but she was confident that if Amondi resisted, she'd ask her to link her up with the right man; quite a difficult task.

Trailing Amondi with a bucket swinging from her arm on their way to the stream, she leaped forward and whispered to Amondi in her rasping voice.

"Please tell me, where does that man come from?"

"Which man?" Amondi asked with a smile.

"The guy who drank excess *andiwo* on your husband's big day."

Amondi burst into loud laughter and looked at Achola with a question mark on her face.

"What about him?" she asked.

"No, I've just asked because he was...*ginene*...okay, I don't know...but just tell me."

"Did you see the second home after our home?" Amondi asked.

"Yes! You mean the big spacious home with a fig tree behind the fence?"

"Exactly! I'll call him on our way back to greet you," Amondi promised.

"Totty!" Amondi shouted with a well-balanced bucket of water on her head on their way back uphill.

"Tottyyyh!" Amondi called out more loudly.

The guy in his village attire emerged from a gap in the fence. He jumped over and hugged Achola with a force that shook the bucket on her head, splashing water all over her clothes.

"I tell you, Amondi, you're a wonderful sister-in-law! You mean you've brought this girl here?…Wah!"

Tears of joy flooded Totty's face as he awkwardly kissed Achola on her lips, cheeks and even down to her neck.

"She'll not go back! Come drought come rain this girl will not go back to Nyakonja," Totty swore.

He escorted the two relatives to Audi's house and started pleading like an idiot with Audi and his wife: "Please allow me to go with her!"

But Amondi responded with a rebuff: "Our girls are not stones to be picked as easily as you feel."

"Okay. What should I do?" Totty asked.

"First, you have to make a public declaration that you want to make her your life partner. Secondly, we must hear from her whether she's interested or not. And, finally, we must organise for a day of launching my cousin to her matrimonial house, not necessarily a big party but a little ceremony where we'll involve your kinsmen to know the wife of their son! Not just sneaking into your house like a cat creeping to steal *omena*. OK?"

239

Amondi declared this without touching on VCT despite her misgivings about ignoring the test; she knew the weaknesses of the two individuals. Ignoring VCT was a shot-cut to a sunset honeymoon…"but…anyway…leave it to God," she shrugged.

"I'll slaughter even a bull if you want but kindly let me hear from this beauty from Nyakonja village in Alego," Totty requested.

"I am still ambivalent about marriage, but I'll think about it overnight and communicate to you my decision tomorrow," Achola said, twiddling with her nails and bending her neck in the village style while responding. She cleared her throat of any grit that would portray her as arrogant or ugly.

The red alcoholic hue in her eyes was unavoidable. Totty accepted her as she was. At the back of her mind, she was thanking God for considering her when she had been pushed to the edge. But she'd give a bad portrait of herself if she accepted Totty's proposal with alacrity. "A good girl worth her salt must show some pride when approached with a marriage proposal to prove that she's not as cheap as somebody may assume," Akuom used to say back home, as an important teaching to growing girls.

"Where is my girl from Alego?" Okwany, Totty's dad popped in and asked Audi immediately after they had just taken supper.

"Here she's," Audi responded, his lips unveiling two rows of huge spade like teeth.

"My girl, how are you?" Okwany shook hands with Achola.

"Fine thank you, Dad," Achola said, bowing respectfully.

"I want you to-to-to join my family," Okwany stammered. He was afraid that Audi's family would tell Achola something bad about Totty or his entire family.

"I've no problem, Dad! I told Totty to wait until tomorrow; I'll give him a feedback then," Achola answered.

Achola heard some piti-piti commotions outside within the compound of the homestead before falling asleep on a mattress spread on the floor of Audi's sitting room but was cautious about sharing it with her cousin the following day in regard to Totty's revelation that he could be Amondi's father-in-law, probably rehearsing in his compound before going places to bewitch people. Family secrets had to be treated with tight lips.

***

"Old man, can I come in?" Amondi knocked Okwany's door in the morning hours of the following day.

"Yes, daughter. Welcome please," said Okwany, ushering Amondi in.

Totty heard Amondi's voice and joined them.

"Thank you, Totty, for coming," Amondi appreciated, sitting down on a chair.

"Now, I've come to deliver my cousin's decision."

"Yes," the old man and his son said, nodding their assents jointly.

"My cousin has accepted Totty's proposal, but on a few conditions," Amondi said and proceeded:

- ➤ Her body is weak and she doesn't want a wife batterer.
- ➤ Totty to be modest in his drinking habits.
- ➤ Totty to be faithful to her as she'll be faithful to him

"It's okay, Totty. You've heard, and I want you to swear, with your own mouth, that you'll live up to those conditions," Okwany turned his face to Totty's side and said, vigorously shaking his head to demonstrate strictness.

"Sincerely, I swear that I will," Totty swore.

***

A tribe of natives was belching with satisfaction in the distant land after celebrating at a goat party organised two days later to establish Achola in her own matrimonial house, at least placing her poles apart from those who were still playing cat and mouse games with insolent stone throwers back in the village. *Tho!* Pong' was good as much as he was mad; there were some cases where he deserved praises.

Back home, Akuota had launched a search for her daughter, whose whereabouts could not be traced. Amondi was in no hurry to take the message back home that the girl was married to her brother-in-law. This was a reaction to circumstances surrounding her disappearance.

"Maybe, my daughter drowned in River Fuludhi!" Akuota wailed in grief. "Maybe she took poison and died somewhere in a thick forest, Oh my God! I could be eating here while wildbeasts are feasting on my daughter's body, Oh my God! Maybe she hanged herself with a rope from a tall tree, *mayie!* My daughter, why can't you send me a dream! I never said you were killing your brother; it's the villagers who had said so! You left all your belongings behind! That's a clear sign of going to kill yourself! But why couln't you leave even a message! Oh, my girl!"

Akuota moaned all day long without resting. She lost her wits, foraging around in all corners of the village with her hands clasped together on her head.

She developed a mental condition that sent Ogoma tumbling head-first into another sunset honeymoon. He moved to a home across the stream, where a rosier fifty-one-year-old widow had not been inherited. Akuota had no time to entertain a stranger when her daughter was nowhere to be seen and her son was bed ridden.

243

Akuota woke up at dawn and trekked to Ng'iya market, where a drover had spotted Achola on a market day.

The guy couldn't talk to her in the hubbub because he was goading a big herd of cattle which could stray if he diverted attention from them to reach out to Achola. He explained that she looked healthier and soberer, clad in new clothes.

But Akuota's woes doubled upon reaching Ng'iya market. The owner of the tin kicked by Akoko more than a year earlier was out and about.

She learnt with a shock that a stranger was stalking her, claiming to be her inheritor.

"This woman kicked my tin and ran away. She's my wife! This woman kicked my tin and ran away. She's my wife!" the crooked old man with heavy jowls, mouth dripping, pressed on until Akuota screamed for help.

But only a trickle of spectators seemed to be willing to help in a society where the rights of such a tin owner were well understood.

"Take her home!" a mad man in the market, who behaved like Pong', shouted.

It was by the grace of God that Oura, the drudge who had ushered Akuota to the medicineman's home once upon a time, was in the same

244

market. He commanded the inheritor with a voice that struck his spine like thunder: "Stop it! Old man!" he ordered. "Do you know this woman? If you want to smell your grave now, go ahead!" The old man in question disintegrated into a coward and vanished in the crowd.

Akuota couldn't explain how it all came about, but it was the influence of money. Money caused Judas Iscariot to betray Jesus. The tin owner had bribed one of the drovers from Nyakonja village plying their trade in the same market to help him identify a woman by the name Akuota any time she went to the market.

The hapless widow lost hope in her pursuit for a lost daughter. She sent Oura with a message to take to the medicineman, who gave her the pig-bone and retired to her home with a conclusion that the man who had seen Achola in the market must have seen a ghost.

Akondo warned Akuota against rushing into performing the rituals done to a person who died in such mysterious circumstances like suicide, drowning or even self poisoning. If at all there was enough evidence to prove that Achola was a victim, Akuota had to organise for a ghost burial ceremony in line with the custom: cut a banana stem, pack it in a coffin and bury it.

Ogoma-Achola protection charms flew Achola's jurisdiction like birds fleeing a dragon infested tree. Her pig-bone had long fallen off her waist in a manner she couldn't understand. She just felt a cool breeze blowing a wound on her right hip, caused by constant scratching by the sharp point of the pig-bone. In her left armpit was a circular scar caused by vigorous brushing of the rim of the round-shaped magic shell.

CHAPTER TWENTY

Ombwede would have smiled all the way to his grave if the wealth used to facilitate his funeral had been spared for upkeep of his orphaned boys and widow. The stench emanating from his casket was a clear sign of reaction against Okebe's decision to offer for funeral services money worth maintaining his family for decades, if the money was given to Achando to invest in some business, for example.

The cost of the suit in which his body was dressed was enough to buy iron sheets for Achando's second house to at least relieve her of the stress of a leaking ten-by-ten inches grass thatched hut.

The money used for buying the coffin in which his body laid was enough for Achando to start some paraffin business that would sustain her and her sons, Othiwi and Akula. If the bull offered by Osweta to be slaughtered for mourners had been sold, she would have gotten capital to start a hotel at Kobare market.

Crocodile tears shed by salivating wife inheritors were meant to lull Achando into believing that Ombwede's death was not a big loss. Individuals were there to refill the gap. They wailed and ran around the compound, throwing themselves to the ground, rubbing their bellies on

247

the ground in the guise of expressing condolence. Deep at the bottoms of their hearts, however, their grief was a charade, the loss was a window of opportunity! They were rubbing their hands in glee. The gorgeous, figure-eight, gleaming Achando was out for grabs.

They worked tirelessly, their bodies reeky of sweat that flooded their bodies from head to toes. They pampered her with dozens of condolence messages. They sang lullabies to baby Othiwi.

But the controversial Pentecostal preacher, endowed with a pair of satellite dishes in the name of ears, planted his assets at the centre of village gossip. He ascended to the podium armed with the right weapons for wife inheritors eyeing the youthful widow:

"Today! As we mourn our dear brother who has left us prematurely, notorious wife inheritors are here, swallowing spoonfuls of saliva for the widow left behind! Believe me if you visit Achando a fortnight from today, you'll find them expressing their desires in hushed tones! Praise the Lord!"

"Yeminaaah (Amen)!" the believers yelled.

Armstrong, the counselor, who frequented Achando's hut in his field activities, never revealed his experiences with the family to the public. He could not, in regard to code of ethics. But he advised the community to accept HIV drugs as the solution to positive living.

At the back of his mind, he knew he had been handling a couple of divided personalities. Achando obeyed his instructions while Ombwede had scoffed at him and stuck to the belief that AIDS is a form of *chira*, which Achwiya was capable of treating. His last words minutes before the angel of death unhooked his soul had been a cursing remark sent to Achola: "She has killed me, tell her to take care of my family if at all she's still alive!"

Armstrong put it clear that he was not an enemy of culture but was against negative, retrogressive cultural practices that fuel the spread of the sexually transmitted infection.

***

A desolate Achando sat in front of her hut pondering her next move a week after burial of her soulmate. With her eyes fixed to the grave where Ombwede's body lay six feet down the earth, she shivered from fear of grappling with the vagaries of losing a husband at such a young age.

Her sparkling, hairless head glittered in the sunlight like the new iron sheets on the roof of Adongo's house after she had faced Achwiya's razor that sloughed off her beautiful lustrous hair in accordance with the custom. She knew she was not an angel to live the rest of her life without a man, but her value had deteriorated. She had no choice but to say yes to any Tom, Dick and Harry who could sail her through cultural road blocks.

Achando wept bitterly the day Pong', of all the people, shed off his madness attire and dressed in a pair of creased, second hand trousers, a clean, torn shirt and a pair of squelching tattered shoes to approach her for some private talks. She was busy doing her domestic chores when the village psycho sneaked in through the fence and entered her hut at dusk.

His dressing style and humble approach rose Achando's shackles even before he spoke out his intentions.

"How can I help you, dear?" Achando asked curiously.

"I just want to be here."

"Tell me please, why you want to be here."

"Just to be here, like Ombwede," Pong' answered with an unusual, low tone.

The bewildered widow in her wisdom offered Pong' a chunk of roast meat and requested him to leave.

Achando was not aware that several widows in the village had secretly lured Pong' to their houses for cultural reasons after failing to win sane wife inheritors, an act that had whetted his appetite for more.

Nasty things were done to widows who had not gone through cleansing processes, like warning men against remarrying them; and, worst, when they died, locking their bodies in private rooms with professional wife inheritors to do unholy acts in the name of fulfilling cultural requirements.

Achando's painful experience of a mad man trying to seduce her followed her to her dream the same night: Herding Akuota's only cow in front of her gate, an ugly scenario of Ombwede beating Pong' at the same spot where he once trounced Omogo emerged. Punching Pong's face and every part of his body, gesticulating wildly and warning his opponent with a rare sound that could only be heard when he was heartbroken. Achando's attempt to separate them hit a snag when the brooding looks on Ombwede's angry face repelled her away.

Foaming at the mouth and pleading desperately, Achando could hardly grasp a word from Pong's burbling plea. All she could hear at the end of every remark was her name - Achando. Ombwede was also giving warnings that ended with question tags quoting the same name, "…Achando! OK?" a clear proof that she was the cause of the fight. Pong' took to his heels when Ombwede turned round to pick a stick for further beating.

"Bind him!" the scared Achando cursed as she bounced back to life. She chucked her blanket and sprang to a sitting position, her chin propped in her palms. She spent a better part of the night in the same position occasionally wiping trickles of tears from her eyes and fretting about a nightmare she could not decipher.

Achando wondered what would have happened could she have allowed Pong' to spend the night in the hut. Ombwede's spirits would haunt her to death.

***

"Is it a ghost or my sister-in-law?" Achando asked in shock, tears of joy flooding her face. She ran at a foot-breaking speed to meet Achola from the gate.

Together with Akuota who joined her, they hugged Achola and gave her kisses that assured the prodigal daughter of her security back home.

Achola had developed cold feet on receiving the news of her brother's death, until Amondi, who had been present on the burial day, assured her that her mother and sister-in-law were regretting the false accusations that had ousted her from her father's home.

"Oh! My girl! Tell me please, why you left us and where you've been!" said Akuota, hyperventilating as she welcomed Achola back home.

"I am married to Audi's cousin."

"Yeah! Yeah! Yeah! Who's this? And how did it come about?"

"He accompanied Audi on his day of eating the sacred hen. If you can remember the guy who gulped down a whole glass of *andiwo*," Achola reminded her mother.

"OK, I remember he and you walked together behind us at the time we were escorting Audi. I am happy the words you were exchanging in hushed tones delivered such colourful results," Achando mused with a chuckle.

"Yeah! I can remember he introduced himself as Samuel." Akuota strained to remember the name of her son-in-law.

"Back home, they call him Totty," Achola revealed.

"But why couldn't you let me know, daughter? I almost killed myself."

"But Mama, can you remember I was on the verge of community wrath if Ombwede had died in my presence?"

"Sorry for that but let's forget about the past and focus ahead. I just wonder why Amondi didn't tell me about your whereabouts when she came here to attend Ombwede's burial."

"She couldn't because she was not happy either about the way I was treated before escaping to my matrimonial home."

"Imagine, somebody told me that he saw you at Ng'iya market."

"It's true I went there to buy a cooking pot for my kitchen."

253

"And how do you see your husband and his family? Are they good people?"

"He's the only one left in their family. They were five boys but four others died from AIDS related infections."

"What do you mean? Is it AIDS or *chira*?"

"His brothers hooked up with widows in the village, who are suspected to have infected them. They never got married but ventured in wife inheritance."

Akuota's face shriveled at her daughter's remarks. "When you left this place," she said, "you were a staunch believer in culture. Now you've come back talking another language."

"Yes, I'm convinced that AIDS is real," Achola declared.

"Have you abandoned your culture?"

"No, I can't abandon our culture. I'm just against negative cultural practices that fuel the spread of HIV."

"Which cultural practices are these?" Akuota asked.

"Irresponsible sex oriented cultural practices," she said, proceeding to enumerate them.

1. For you to launch a new house even if you don't have a husband, you have to look for any man and have unprotected sex with him in the house as is the custom.

254

2. If your man dies, like Ombwede has, people will force Achando to have unprotected sex with a man whose HIV status she doesn't know to fulfill customary requirements before remarrying.

3. At the dawn of a new season just before sowing seeds in your farms, you start by engaging in sex oriented cultural practices. If you don't have a husband, you look for a man whose HIV status you don't know, with whom to do the same.

Achola looked more enlightened and exposed than she had been before getting married. Here was a totally new she, extremely pregnant with Totty's unborn baby, sweetened by marriage, with a better sense of dignity and self-worth. Her red alcoholic eyes had been swabbed clean by family responsibilities and her endeavour to maintain a good portrait of herself in her matrimonial home. Totty was not interested in a drunkard as his wife, as much as he was a drunkard himself.

"And where is my step-father?" Achola asked.

"That lout? I chased him away. He now lives with another widow across the stream."

"That's good."

Akuota's house was cramped by villagers celebrating the return of their girl after fear that she had committed suicide. Special cleansing activities would have had to be done had Akuota hurried to perform the ghost burial ceremony only to realise later that she was alive.

"Do you have people walking around like Armstrong in your village?" Akuota asked.

"Yes, they tested me and my husband and nowadays it's a routine for us to be tested on monthly basis. The only point of contention in regard to *chira* and AIDS is irresponsible sexual behaviour in the name of fulfilling cultural requirements."

With the label of *okola* etched on her forehead, Achando's movements remained confined to her hut and Akuota's house. Village folks would scamper to safety if she entered somebody's home before performing all the rites.

It was taboo for Ogoma to sail Achando through because he had lived with her mother-in-law for quite sometime. Akuota quickly killed and roasted her hen to give Achola as a gift for her husband. Her departure would give them some breathing space because her AIDS gospel was cramping their cultural activities at that time that she wanted to help her daughter-in-law to maneuver her way through the rituals. After all, she was happy that Achola was alive and safe.

The next culprit was Omogo but there were two issues to consider: first, Omogo was living with Akoko, who had shared Ogoma with her mother-in-law. That would sow grievous seeds of disasters if Achando made a mistake of allowing him to spend in the late Ombwede's hut.

Secondly Omogo's face was scuffed by beatings from the late Ombwede, although that was a minor issue because they had reconciled at the time of Ombwede's death.

Achando rued the day she pounced on Okong'o and trounced him like a toddler. He would have been the best ladder to climb from the pit of the mucky *okola* issue.

"Kindly advise me. The next issue is getting an inheritor, and I am stranded," Achando consulted Akuota.

"The right man would be Okong'o, but remember the day you deflated his ego by beating him like a child," Akuota reminded her.

"I'll try to apologize and lure him," Achando said.

"It's okay. Okong'o is easy to handle if you can offer him presents. He's a sot; I'll offer him free drinks. But remember, you have to be secretive; otherwise, Akuru will go berserk," Akuota advised.

"Thank you, Mama," Achando appreciated.

Akuota had long forgotten her doctor's advice against engaging an inheritor soon after burying a deceased husband. No seed of any vegetation had germinated on Ombwede's grave and there she was, advising her daughter-in-law on how to clinch an inheritor.

Wearing a dreamy smile on her face, Achando wandered around Akuru's home, casting glances in her compound from a safe vantage to signal Okong'o if she could spot him. She carried a bunch of firewood on her arm to cheat prying eyes that she was fetching firewood.

"What's wrong with this woman? Can't she give her man a breathing space?" Achando muttered to herself when her eyes caught up with Okong'o, walking side by side with Akuru, whispering to each other ear to ear.

Achando surrendered and walked back home. But she remained optimistic. She and her mother-in-law conjured a charming approach that would work better. They decided to hook Okong'o in the afternoon of that day when Akuru was expected to be in the market selling her baskets.

Akoko, who was tipped on the plan, crossed Akuru's fence when she saw her back on the main road, heading to the village open air market.

"You look bored!" said Akoko, her charming smile tickling Okong'o, who sprang from his seat in the shade to meet her.

"I don't have even a coin for *andiwo*," Okong'o complained.

"Let's go to Akuota's den, I'll convince her to lend me a glass of the same," she said to him.

Prickled with excitement, Okong'o accompanied Akoko to Akuota's house, where he was offered a glass of the grog but he was too strong and agile to be tricked in the manner a woman had been forced to Osweta's house. Some kind of negotiations would suffice.

The three women involved the wife inheritor in a conclave, where they freely aired their grievances.

"But Achando fought me one day in this compound as if I were Othiwi," Okong'o complained.

"Forgive me, dear. I did it out of stupidity. Achola, who had incited me, is no longer with us," Achando apologised.

"It's okay. I'll cheat her that I'm joining my friends for a drink here and come at night," Okong'o promised.

4am local time, Akuru was wriggling in her bed with anxiety over her lover's whereabouts. He couldn't be at his home because Adongo had launched the main house with an adulterous ghost.

She thought of penetrating the inky darkness to his home but the fear of meeting Ratila on the way stopped her. Maybe, she thought, he had decided to sleep in Adongo's kitchen.

It was alright, according to her, if by any means he had made his way back to his home after using an antidote from Achwiya. But it would be a death sentence if it was the case of another woman, different from Adongo, engaging Okong'o in a romantic relationship. She clicked her tongue and muttered some ancient Luo curses.

Two hours was too long for her to wait. She sprang out of her bed and pried the door open. She walked up and down her compound brandishing her stick for the day's tussle but fled back to her house for safety at the sight of a huge bushy human figure prominently running past her gate - piti-piti-piti-piti-piti-piti, possibly, Ratila racing back home after a hard night's work.

Akuru ran around the village like a dog on heat when the day broke. She flinched at the sight of Adongo, who was working in her potato farm in front of her home, and made a U-turn to a safer vantage from where she could safely view Adongo's home if at all Okong'o had spent the night there but found it colourless, she only saw Okong'o's children winnowing beans. She sped uphill towards Osweta's home and vented her spleen on Akwede, who intercepted her.

"Leave me alone and go your way! Woman!" she snarled.

"No, I can't let you go before you tell me your problem; you could be up to committing suicide," Akwede insisted.

"Imagine, Okong'o has gone missing!" she moaned.

"Lazy woman! The man is enjoying a happy moment with Achando," Akwede revealed with a chuckle.

"Why does he go to a woman who sat upon his chest and beat him like a stray dog?" Akuru reacted.

Akuru braced for a fierce battle with the widow but a sense of security struck the back of her mind. She assessed the forces surrounding Achando and cringed with fear.

The two notorious names, Akuota and Akoko, could not be underrated by anybody preparing for a battle. Their lunatic gimmicks were enough to pulverise Akuru even before they touched her. They owned the drink that Okong'o would rather die than spend a day without tasting.

Being the only girl in a family of seven, Achando would call for backup from her brothers back home if Akuru by any means defeated the two women. They had what it takes to give Okong'o all the luxuries he needed for maintenance purposes.

Akuota and Akoko charged their brains with alcohol in the morning purposely to yell taunts at the hapless Akuru.

They wandered around the village chanting the victory slogan: "Achando and Okong'o are like hinge and door! Jealous woman kill yourself!"

Akuru felt scared at the sight of the two drunken women walking towards her on a narrow path with cheeky grins on their faces.

"Aheheeeeh! Auh!" they burst into loud *fwan* laughter after meeting her without a single word of greeting.

"Somebody rejoiced when receiving gold; she's now saddened by the loss of the rare commodity!" Akoko yelled in parables.

Normalcy was restored after realising that Akuru had conceded defeat. She resorted to consulting Akondo for a more humane settlement of the issue.

"Kindly talk to Akuota and Akoko. They're too much on me since they snatched away my man," Akuru complained.

"Why do you refer to Okong'o as your man?" Akondo, seated on a stool in front of his *duol*, asked with some arrogance in his voice.

"We've been with him for quite some time," Akuru claimed.

"Okong'o is a freelance wife inheritor. He's free to go anywhere to help a widow in need," Akondo corrected. "Don't claim ownership of a bird simply because it has perched on the rooftop of your house...girl!"

"But you know,'' Akuru complained, "Achando started frustrating me way back in those days when Swale was still alive."

"What do you mean? Achando is a child of yesterday. How did she frustrate you?" Akondo asked curiously.

"Do you know the biological father to her son Akula?" Akuru asked.

"No please, tell me!" Akondo lowered his tone and positioned his hairy old ear near Akuru's mouth to hear perfectly.

"My late husband sired the boy with her," Akuru revealed.

"You mean?" Akondo screeched in shock.

"Had her mother not apologised to me, I'd have scalded that *hududu fuong'* with hot water," Akuru threatened.

"Please tell me, how did it come about? Your husband was too old for Achando!" Akondo requested with a smile, wondering whether Akuru had the potential to refer to anybody as *hududu fuong'*.

"She enticed him with her charming smile and submissiveness. I discovered when it was already too late that my husband used to pick her from her parents' home at night. Those days that she used to sleep in her mother's kitchen, before she crossed over to your kitchen," Akuru revealed.

"Yes, I can remember she started sleeping in my kitchen after delivering Akula," Akondo confirmed.

"And then he used to sneak with her to his *duol*." Akondo bowed his head in shock at the revelation.

"I was tipped by the same Akoko who's now frustrating me with another man in my love triangle. I hid at the fence near his *duol* after serving him supper and spotted Achando creeping into the private house. I almost killed that prostitute with a spear, but my husband jumped onto my throat and gagged me with death threats if I was tempted to blurb about it, only to discover that she was already pregnant with his child! Her mother visited me the following day with an apology and promised disciplinary action against her daughter," Akuru substantiated.

"Sorry, daughter! Sorry! Our children today get spoilt before they're born. Your man was over fifty years by the time the girl conceived while she was around twenty or nineteen, if I'm not wrong but any way…it's part of life. I'll talk to Akuota and Akoko to avoid embarrassing you in public. Even if they have submerged Okong'o in their romantic well, they should leave you alone," Akondo concluded, sympathy written all over his face.

Akondo summoned the two women later in the day to advise them accordingly, but the brazen sellers of *andiwo* did not hesitate to reveal that the love tussle between the middle aged Akuru and the youthful widow was not an issue of yesterday.

"Achando and Akuru are like the quick brown fox that jumps over the lazy dog," Akoko said with a chuckle.

"Why do you brag like that, Akoko? Can't you handle this case with some respect to your fellow woman?" Akondo pleaded.

"Look here, old man, Akuru should tell us why she slept in class until her husband impregnated Achando. Even I, if I sleep in class, I'll be shocked to learn that Omogo has hooked up with another woman," Akoko said, chuckling. The remark added more evidence to Akuru's claim.

"Why do you reveal that in the presence of Akuota. She'll chase away Akula to go and reclaim his share of Swale's land.

"What do you think I don't know? It'd be risky if Ombwede were still alive, but now he's dead. We'll expose it to the entire community, who'll help us decide where Akula will build his hut, whether at Swale's home or in Achando's home," Akuota yelled.

"That's too much for me at the moment. I'll probably be dead by then, but my piece of advice as for now is that Akuru is one of us. She's a very humble woman, who depends on basket weaving for her living, kindly treat her with some dignity," Akondo advised.

"We've no problem as long as she doesn't interfere with Ombwede's widow. Even I, released Ogoma and set him free to go and help another widow. A wife inheritor is a godsend messenger to save widows from cultural woes, and nobody is allowed to stick to an inheritor like a tick on the skin of an animal," Akuota responded.

***

Another day of a joint ceremony that brought the community members together was the day of reconciling Apudo to her husband. Owiti's reason for reclaiming his wife was understandable in regard to family security belief that views a boy child as the pillar of his family.

Owiti's new wife had no serious weakness compared to the estranged Apudo. She was loyal, humble, hardworking, submissive and, most important, gorgeous. But a chink in her armour was that she had never delivered a boy child since she got married after the departure of Apudo. Owiti felt it important to reclaim his wife and embrace her weaknesses because her womb blossomed with male children.

Some good but ugly news for Owiti on his arrival to reclaim his wife was that Apudo was breastfeeding a one-month old baby boy sired by the notorious stone throwers who milled around Akondo's homestead every night.

The news was good because the ghost father of the child was a donor. The child's title would be changed to Owiti as soon as he reclaimed his wife the same way the late Ombwede had changed Akula's title to his after marrying Achando. The ugly side of the news was the customary conditions on how to treat an illegitimate child. His house had to be on the left-hand side of the main house facing the gate if he was the first-born like Akula but in this case, he was not, there were two brats in the name of elder brothers sired by Owiti. He had to be absent on the day of establishing their new home. There were a number of other conditions that created a wedge between him and the other family members.

Apudo's family accorded their son-in-law a warm welcome to at least take away his wife and relieve them of the stress caused by her messes with village boys, a habit that portrayed the family in bad light.

The occasion was as ceremonious as Audi's big day. Osweta, who had so far gone senile, didn't attend, leaving only Onyoyo and the groovy Akondo to grace the occasion.

The stern warnings always given to men who mistreat their wives were replaced by some friendly advice by Akondo and Akuom. It was all joy and pleasure to see Apudo back to her matrimonial house to grapple with the vagaries of living with a polygamous husband.

The elders sighed with relief any moment such wonders happened. They whittled down characters that were viewed as burdens to the community, such as mature unmarried idle girls, lousy community members, young unmarried boys getting submerged in wife inheritance craze, some inheriting widows as old as their mothers or even older and engaging in irresponsible drinking habits, and so on. Renunciation of *chira* and accepting of the doctors' advice on prevention and living with HIV/Aids was the way to go. The HIV infection could be controlled by use of condoms and through abstinence or faithfulness to one sexual partner.

The village was reeling from the harbinger of a crisis of grey hair, enriched with wisdom, to bless the seeds of their workmanship. When the young vanish, like smoke in the air, the society shivers, from the gust of wind that rips her shield and breaks her pillars. The sting of a phenomenon that beats our magic and defeats our prophets! The wind from the sea, that sweeps our souls, like ants on the floor. The seer from the skies, stretch forth your arm, to the pillars of the planet, restore their hinges, or else we'll perish. Happy are those liberated from shackles of negative cultural oppression! Amen!

QUIETUS